D1643436

AN AWKWARD LIE

AN AWKWARD LIE

A Bobby Appleby story

by

MICHAEL INNES

LONDON
VICTOR GOLLANCZ LTD
1971

ISBN 0 575 00507 6

PRINTED IN GREAT BRITAIN BY
NORTHUMBERLAND PRESS LIMITED
GATESHEAD

CONTENTS

Part One

THE BUNKER

CHAPTER ONE

Mr Robert Appleby (successful scrum-half retired, and author of that notable anti-novel *The Lumber Room*) fixed his gaze for a full thirty seconds on the flag on the first green. Then, judging that the sudden ghastly threat to his stomach and his bowels had abated, he took another look at the body in the bunker. He might as well make what he could of it (he told himself, as his normal mental processes began to return). It wasn't the sort of thing a man was likely to come on twice.

Or only a man—his own father, for instance—who made such matters his business. Sir John Appleby's earlier career —Bobby Appleby vaguely supposed—had been corpses all the time. But although his father was quite willing to indulge in reminiscence over some of these, he allowed himself a certain fastidiousness in point of gory detail. So Bobby had always been disposed to imagine that when somebody had a bullet directed at his brain the resulting token was one small hole, or perhaps two small holes, in the head. Intellectually, of course, he was better informed. Friends who had done a spot of V.S.O. between university and taking up a job, and who had in consequence stumbled into one or another nasty little war in remote places, had been much less reticent than Sir John about the frequent surprising sheer messiness of homicide. But the present spectacle was his own introduction to anything of the kind. What had happened to this man's head at least seemed to make it certain that he was dead. Quite a bit of it had vanished.

The bunker was large and quite unusually broad. If your

drive had been entirely to your satisfaction, and some delusion of grandeur persuaded you that you could be snugly beside the pin in two, then this hazard was more likely to get you than not. As a matter of fact, it had got Bobby now. His ball was pretty well in the mathematical centre of the bunker. And so was the dead man. The dead man could (so to speak) have stretched out an arm and put the ball in his pocket.

There was an immediate problem, turning on the fact that Bobby was at present alone on the links. It was his habit, when spending a summer weekend at Long Dream, occasionally to run over to Linger early in the morning and play a practice nine holes before returning to his parents' home for breakfast. It usually made him late for the meal. But nobody minded. Mrs Colpoys enjoyed being vastly put out by Mr Robert—to the extent of keeping something hot in the oven, and allowing him to make fresh coffee in her kitchen. His father, looking up from his reading of *The Times* in the breakfast-room window, would politely inquire whether he had found himself in form, particularly in point of that rather uncertain command of his with a niblick. His mother would sit down at the table for a few minutes with a great air of general gossip, but with what Bobby judged to be the palpable design of suggesting some polite attention to one of the more eligible young gentlewomen of the region. Bobby would make large and disingenuous promises about activity of this sort some months' ahead. On the whole he preferred what his father called Away Matches where girls were concerned.

This morning there would be something altogether more grim to talk about. And meantime there was the problem. Bobby had seen it at once.

A bunker on a golf-course is rather a special place within which to find a man who has suffered violent death. It was clear, moreover, that this bunker had been raked over by a green-keeper late on the previous evening. There were a certain number of footprints in the sand. But not very many. And Bobby would add to these the moment he stepped off the turf.

So perhaps he should simply hurry away to the clubhouse and telephone for the police. For the man was *certainly* dead. But what if he wasn't? Or—and this was the real truth of the matter—what if he were? Even from a dead body one doesn't simply turn aside. To go up to it and touch it is the human thing to do. The slightest suspicion of life, of course, and one would run like anything for a doctor. But a dead man one watches by, if possible, until somebody comes along.

These notions, surprisingly old-world in a novelist of the *avant-garde*, passed quite quickly through Bobby's mind. It was as a result of them that he now stepped carefully into the bunker, treading only where the sand was still wholly undisturbed. He knelt beside the body. That meant an indentation made by his left knee, but again he wasn't obliterating anything. The dead man lay prone and with his face in the sand. Bobby's first thought was that you couldn't tell how old he was. Not even by the colour of the hair on the back of the head. What had killed him had seen to that.

The dead man's jacket looked expensive. It was made of a good Lovat tweed. Bobby put out a hand and touched it. It felt slightly damp. But there had been no rain since Bobby woke up at about seven o'clock, and he thought it improbable that there had been any during the night. What had produced this damp feeling was dew. Perhaps the body had been lying here throughout the night. Bobby remembered that it is on cold surfaces that moisture condenses as dew. He slipped his hand under the dead man's jacket. Overcoming a certain reluctance, he pulled up the dead man's shirt-tail to his waist and slipped his hand gently beneath it, so that his palm lay on the naked flesh of the dead man's back. The body was very cold. For a confused fraction of a second Bobby felt this to be unnatural. It was as if the man's clothing had been falling down on its job. Then he realised that this was how a dead body felt—how it felt when a certain interval of time had elapsed since death. He didn't at all know—as his father would—what that interval of time would be. It must vary, he supposed, according to one circumstance or another. He realised that he ought to look at his watch. But his watch was on the wrist of the hand that lay on this lately living thing which had chilled to clay. For a moment he fumbled once more with the dead man's shirt-tail, shoving it back under the waist-band of his trousers. It seemed a necessary thing to do—just because the man *was* dead and could never know indignity again. Then his hand came free, and he saw that it was ten minutes to eight. Quite often there were other people out on the course by this time—either after an early breakfast or doing as Bobby himself had proposed to do. But now there was nobody around.

The club-house, naturally, wasn't all that far away from the first green. But a small spinney—it made the first hole a dog's-leg affair—had edged it out of view. It probably wasn't beyond shouting range, particularly as the morning was very still. But the mere stillness somehow made Bobby reluctant to start hallooing, and in any case there hadn't appeared to be anybody around. He remembered that the labour force of the golf club consisted of two men and a boy, and that they all lived not even in Linger itself, but in the little clump of council houses close to Linger Junction. The club's professional, although he spent most of his time either in the club-house or on the course, had recently attained to rather a grand little villa more than a mile away. None of these people probably arrived until half-past eight or thereabouts. So in default of another matutinal player turning up, Bobby would have to keep his wake by the body for some time. He decided that, after

12

all, the most sensible thing would be to return to the club-house and telephone the local police.

He straightened up, and backed out of the bunker just as he had come. He did this so precisely that the effect was odd; it was as if a heavy man had walked up to the body, knelt by it, and then been snatched into the air by a balloon, a helicopter, a demon, or a guardian angel. This fancy made Bobby pause when he had reached the grass— this in order to take a synoptic view of such other evidence of this kind as the surface of the bunker afforded. But— inevitably, perhaps—his glance was first drawn back once more to the body.

Once you had recovered from the mere gruesomeness of the spectacle—it occurred to him—your main impression was of its dramatic quality. Here, surely, was somebody who had been ruthlessly shot down as he fled. The man's legs were splayed out in a manner suggesting just that. His left arm lay beneath his head, as if he had flung it up to protect his face as he fell. His right arm was stretched stiffly out from his side. It was as if he really were trying to reach for Bobby's ball. Or perhaps it was not quite like that—for the hand was bent back at the wrist, and the thumb and fingers were spread out wide, and slightly crooked, like the hand of a man who makes a last desperate clutch at empty air. Bobby looked at this hand. And suddenly, without his at first at all knowing why, a queer cold tremor ran down his spine. And it was doing this—the persuasion was at once utterly illogical and wholly over-whelming—not now but a long time ago.

The feeling was one which Robert Appleby had never experienced before. A fraction of a second passed, and it had modulated into one which was almost comfortably familiar although inexpugnably strange. It was a feeling known as *déjà vu*. Just this had happened long ago. Looking at that hand. And the shiver. Or the *frisson*. (Mr Robert Appleby, anti-novelist and admirer of Monsieur

13

Robbe-Grillet, very oddly—even to his own sense—took time off to reflect upon the superiority of the French tongue.) Bobby also noticed that he was *frightened*. It was that sort of shiver (or *frisson*). He had glimpsed something which had once frightened him very much.

But now something had happened to the body. The morning sunlight (although he hadn't consciously noted this) had been at play upon it. This remained true only of the three extended limbs. The rest of the dead man's body was in shadow. And the shadow was the shadow of a human being. Bobby turned round, and saw the girl.

'Has your friend had an accident?' The girl asked this in a calm sort of way. But not in a cold way. She was humanly concerned. Because she was between Bobby and the sun still low on the horizon, he was less aware of her features than of her figure. Her face was in shadow. Her body, through what seemed a flimsy dress, was very much in silhouette. Bobby was momentarily disturbed by this. Being (as has been remarked) somewhat old-fashioned in some of his instincts, he believed in faces first and figures later: this rather than the other way about. He had a sudden strong wish—surprising in the present harassing situation—simply to *see* this girl; to observe her features, her expression, clearly, and thus know what she looked like. What are vulgarly called a woman's vital statistics may be arresting, but they can't honestly be termed in-formative. A voice, on the other hand, can. Bobby was a good deal struck by the girl's voice.

'He isn't a friend,' Bobby said. 'And I don't think he's had an accident. Or not what you could call an accident. I think he's killed himself—or that somebody has killed him.'

'You mean you've never seen him before? You've just stumbled upon him?'

'I haven't done any stumbling.' Bobby didn't quite know

14

why he produced this absurdly literal reply. 'But that's my ball in the bunker. I simply walked up, and there he was.'

'A stranger?' It was rather sharply that the girl seemed to put this question.

'I didn't say that. I said not a friend.' Bobby felt that he was talking rather stupidly. Perhaps he was suffering from what they called shock. 'I've a queer notion that I knew him long ago.'

'He's not going to be much helped by that.' As well as being calm, the girl's voice was now critical. 'Hadn't we better get some help?'

'Well, yes. But not help for *him*. He's quite dead. I thought I'd told you that.' Bobby took a few steps away from the bunker. There was no reason why he shouldn't get a clearer view of this girl who had sprung from nowhere. 'Do you live round about here?'

'Not very much.' The girl didn't make this sound a very evasive reply. 'Do you?'

'More or less. My parents live at a place called Long Dream. It's on the other side of Linger.' Bobby, turning to face the girl, now had the sun behind him. He had a momentary sense—wholly indecorous in the circumstances —that here at last was *his* girl. He told himself hastily that the same persuasion had on quite a number of occasions visited him before, and that nothing whatever had come of it. 'I wonder,' he said briskly, 'if you would mind going and making a telephone call?'

'For a doctor, you mean? Or for the police?'

'Both, I suppose.'

'I think that you had better do that.' The girl had turned on the corpse a glance that was level and unalarmed. 'You know who's who, I suppose. I'll stay here.'

'I'd hardly like to think—'

'Don't be stupid, please. I'm not in a hurry. And a dead man—you say he *is* dead—isn't going to hurt me. Is there a telephone in that club-house?'

'Yes, of course.'

'Then go and get on with it.' The girl had produced a packet of cigarettes. 'You won't mind if I smoke?'

'Why on earth should I? Because it's unwomanly?' Rather belatedly, Bobby tumbled to the girl's meaning. 'A dead man's in no position to mind. So it's up to you.'

'Then here goes.' The girl struck a match. 'But you will come back when you've telephoned? I don't think I want to be found alone here by a posse of policemen.'

'Of course I'll come back. I don't expect I'll be ten minutes.'

'Then go about it now.' The girl seemed to inhale her cigarette deeply. 'But what you said about knowing him long ago. Have you—well, turned over the body and looked at him?'

'No, I haven't. One oughtn't to do that, when a man has died in this way. But there's something that one can see now—just as he lies there.' Bobby hesitated. He hadn't meant by this to suggest that the girl should scrutinize the corpse. A single glimpse must surely have been shocking enough. He saw now, however, that she was continuing to gaze at it dispassionately. It was possible that she had turned pale under the impact of this horrible experience, but her complexion was very fair, and he couldn't be sure. He could be sure that she wasn't insensitive. Her composure was the result of effort. So, for that matter, was his.

'Something one can see?' The girl had taken up Bobby's remark incisively. 'That tells you you've seen him long ago?'

'It's his right index-finger.'

'You are very observant. I hadn't noticed.' Now the girl was looking away—out over the golf-course. It was as if this last small thing was more physically discomposing than everything else. Bobby had felt the same. But then Bobby had a particular reason for it. 'Perhaps,' the girl added, 'I thought it was just curled up. If I thought anything at all.'

'It may be coincidence. I think perhaps I *will* have a look. I can just turn the head a very little.'

'Why not?' The girl seemed almost amused. 'One mustn't be squeamish. Go ahead.' She had moved to the farther lip of the bunker, and so was on a higher level than Bobby. 'I can see somebody,' she said. 'No, it's a couple of people. On the verge of the road. Shall I go and disturb their picnic?'

'People don't picnic at this hour of the morning.' Bobby —rather carefully watching where he put his feet again— walked round the bunker to join her. 'Are you sure?'

'Perhaps it's not the technical word. They have a cara- van—a trailer. It's their breakfast.'

'And they run to a pretty powerful car.' The appearance which the girl had spotted was really too far off to be made much of, and it was only from this slightly more elevated perch that it was visible at all. 'They look as if they were packing up,' Bobby said. 'And I'm fairly sure we oughtn't to let them go. Or not without getting the number of their car. It's just possible they may have seen something that's important in this business. I'll sprint over to them.'

'I'll do that. I don't run too badly. And if they do get on their way, they're more likely to stop at a wave from a girl than a man. And you get off to the telephone. The ... the corpse can look after itself for the inside of ten minutes.'

'Right!' It seemed to Bobby there was sense in this. 'If they're not co-operative, scare them with the police.'

Hardly waiting for this last injunction, the girl turned and ran. It was true that this was something she knew how to do. For a brief moment Bobby watched her. Then he himself swung round and made for the club-house.

He remembered as he ran that he hadn't, after all, man- aged to glimpse the features of the dead man. So he didn't yet know—although he must do soon—whether it could really, by some amazing chance, be Bloody Nauze who was lying in the bunker. Nauze (whose name rhymed with 'rose') had always been called that—partly because of the joke and partly because he *was* bloody. Although he couldn't, that was to say, have been called with the slightest fairness a pathological sadist (supposing small boys to have been able to command such an expression), he had certainly been much too free with a gym-shoe to be an agreeable feature of a private school. Bobby had heard of this propensity of Bloody Nauze during his first night in dorm. He hadn't, he seemed to recall, been a particularly timid infant. On the other hand, since he had never once been hit up to that point in his young life, he had no means of estimating how much a gym-shoe would hurt. He had therefore been alarmed, on the following morning, to learn that Mr Nauze was going to be responsible for guiding his first steps in the Latin tongue. Looking back later, Bobby had never had any inclination to suppose that it had been other than a mild and compassable alarm. But perhaps, in an instantly suppressed sort of way, it had really been a wild terror. For that was what he felt when Bloody Nauze suddenly shouted and pointed at him. The man had merely shouted 'Next boy!' when in quest of something like the genitive plural of *mensa*. And he had pointed at Bobby similarly without any sinister intent. Bobby *was* the next boy, and he had simply wanted to make that fact rapidly clear. But—had it been for seconds, or had it been for a whole day?—Bobby had been really bothered. He had been really bothered (he had imagined) at being pointed at with an index-finger which wasn't there.

It wasn't the action—Bobby, a child of precociously reflective habit, had soon concluded—of what you could call a well-regulated mind. The chap did, after all, have a left hand, and why couldn't he use that? He'd used it for the gym-shoe. Not that that had turned out, after all, much to darken Bobby's days. Bobby had ended up getting on rather well with Bloody Nauze. For one thing, the chap had taught Latin admirably.

But all that had been at least twelve years ago. Bobby almost slackened his pace to a more elderly sort of run as this shocking fact was borne in upon him. If you could look back a dozen years like that, then in no time you would be looking back twenty or forty. His parents were fond of doing just that in their table-talk, and sometimes he had to repress an irrational panic as he listened. *Devouring Time, blunt thou the lion's paws*. That sort of feeling.

There still seemed to be not a soul around the club-house, and to get to the telephone he had to let himself in with his father's key. He himself was only some sort of guest-member, and hadn't a key of his own. But he had no difficulty about making the call, since there was a public telephone just inside the entrance. Bobby dialled 999—which meant, he supposed, that he didn't even have to pay. And he got through to the police station immediately. He thought he had better begin by identifying himself.

'My name's Appleby,' Bobby said.

'Yes, Sir John.' The voice at the other end was rather notably brisk and alert.

'No, that's my father. Robert Appleby.'

'Yes, Mr Appleby.' This time, the voice suggested a relaxed attention.

'I'm speaking from the club-house on the golf-course. I've found a dead man. In a bunker.'

'Found a dead man.' Now the voice indicated transcription in long-hand into a notebook. 'In a bunker.' There was a pause. 'Are you sure he's dead, sir?'

'Absolutely sure.'

'Very good, sir. We'll be with you in no time.'

'Thank you very much.' Bobby felt obscurely that this colloquy had been a little lacking in drama. 'Ought I to call a doctor?'

'You can leave that to us, sir. And no need to worry.'
The voice had decided to suggest reassurance and even
benevolence. 'Just stay where you are, and we'll contact
you within ten minutes.'

'I rather think I ought to be getting back to the bunker.
There's a young—'

'We'd prefer you to wait for us, Mr Appleby.' For the
first time, the voice was authoritative. 'Remaining by the
instrument from which a call is made cuts out confusion
and often saves time. Routine request, sir.'

'Oh, very well.' Bobby wasn't too pleased, and he felt
suddenly tempted to administer a smart shock. So he
succumbed to decidedly stretching his existing sense of
the situation. 'But it looks like murder, and I've seen some
men preparing to make off in a car. So you'd better hurry
up.'

And Bobby put down the receiver. It wasn't without a
sense that his last effort had been a shade childish. There
hadn't, after all, been the slightest suggestion that the
chap in the police station at Linger had proposed to waste
a moment. And something of the marked courtesy which
he'd noticed his father was careful to employ in any rela-
tions with the country constabulary was no doubt incum-
bent on other Applebys as well. Bobby didn't mean to be
a policeman. But he had a high sense of the eminence to
which his father had attained in that odd walk of life.

So now it occurred to him that he ought to ring up
home and give an account of himself. As this couldn't be
done on 999 he had to fish out some money. But again he
got through quickly. And it was his father who answered.

'It's me,' Bobby said. 'Look—I've found a dead man in
the bunker near the first green. It looks as if somebody
has blown the chap's brains out. So I've sent for the police.'

'Not an excessive response, I'd say, to such a situation.
Shall you be back to breakfast?'

'Yes, I suppose so. Unless they run me in on suspicion

or something.'

'That *would* be excessive.' The voice of Bobby's father dropped carefully to a casual note. 'You all right?'

'Yes, of course.'

'Good—then we'll hear about it at breakfast. By the way, if it's a Sergeant called Howard who comes along, he's a very sound man. Good-bye.'

There was a click, and Bobby too put down the receiver. It hadn't remotely occurred to him that he needed to be, as they say, steadied. But, he thought, steadied he had been. He went outside again—wondering whether, when he did get home, it would be with the astonishing news that Bloody Nauze was the dead man. Meanwhile, if he walked to some point well beyond the first tee, he could probably get a glimpse of the bunker beyond the tip of the spinney. Perhaps he would be able to give the girl a wave. It was odd about the girl. He hadn't learnt her name —nor she his—and there had been about her a curious air of detachment, of floating loose above the local scene.

He was passing the first tee when he heard the telephone ring in the still empty club-house behind him. He hesitated, and decided it might quite well be the police again. Perhaps they had some system of checking up on calls which were possibly no more than attempts at a stupid hoax. So he turned and went back at the double. He had, after all, undertaken to stay put. The call turned out to be a wrong number. When he got outside once more, it was to find a car drawing to a halt in front of him. It was a large black saloon, with one of those little lighthouse-things on the middle of its roof. And it had POLICE written on it, fore and aft, in what immediately suggested itself as the colour of blood. Bobby Appleby, the most blameless of citizens (and a talented writer), felt a wholly irrational twinge of apprehension at the spectacle. A sign of the times, he told himself. A token of the spirit of the age. These were the people who, all over the world, beat up your contemporaries in the streets, tore down their banners, hustled them into vans.

Mr Robert Appleby, admiring son of a retired Police Commissioner, noted in himself with some sobriety this strong if fleeting reaction. Then he stepped forward.

'Sergeant Howard?' he asked politely.

Sergeant Howard it was. He didn't suggest a world in which sinister things happened to you as soon as they got you inside. In a decently restrained way, there was something fatherly about Sergeant Howard. He started off, it was true, with a steady and frankly appraising scrutiny of the young man who had made the telephone call. The effect was the more impressive because Sergeant Howard had eyes of an almost unnaturally light blue. This gave his stare a chilly quality. But if Bobby was alarmed, it was only for a second. He had a sense—perhaps a little too habitual with him, since he was a personable young man— of being, at least provisionally, approved of.

'We'd better get straight to it,' Howard said briskly. 'We' meant Bobby, Howard himself, and a constable who had driven the car. It also looked like meaning several other men who had turned up by now—early-morning golfers who were aware that something strange must have occurred, and who saw no reason why they shouldn't discreetly bring up the rear of the procession. A certain publicity was going to attend the next stage of the affair. 'Where about, sir?' Howard asked.

'Close to the first green. We go round that spinney, and there it is.'

'I think you said something about a car, Mr Appleby. And about some men making an escape in it. We met nothing of the sort as we came from Linger. Of course, they may have made off in the direction of Drool. Did they seem to be armed?'

'Well, no. I think they were having a picnic, as a matter of fact.'

'A picnic?' the constable asked. 'Did you say a picnic, sir?'

'That was what the girl called it. It might have been breakfast. They had a caravan. And a big car—I think a Mercedes.' Bobby felt he wasn't doing too well. 'I didn't mean they actually *looked* like murderers—'

'Mr Appleby, did I understand you to say something about a girl?' It was with an effect almost of curiosity that Sergeant Howard asked this.

'Yes. I don't know who she is. She just walked up. She'll be waiting there now. I hope she'll have persuaded the people with the car to wait as well.'

'Quite a reception committee.' Sergeant Howard said this rather too drily to suggest an attempt at humour. 'Do you know this dead man, Mr Appleby?'

'He's face-downward in the sand, so I can't really say.' Bobby felt he had better out with the astonishing idea in his head. 'But he has the first finger of his right hand missing, and I've known a man like that.'

'I've known several.' Sergeant Howard was extremely unimpressed. 'A very common injury, sir. In the war, for instance. And self-inflicted, as often as not. Do it cleverly enough, and enemy action can't be excluded. Takes a man right out of the line for good.'

'I see.' Bobby was depressed by this professional rapport with human ignobility. He also wondered whether Bloody Nauze's mutilation had been of this order. It was queer to think of a man pointing at you a finger whose non-existence was the consequence of his own cowardice and desperation.

For some moments they walked in silence. Another couple of golfers had joined the march. Bobby wondered with irritation why they couldn't go and start their game, rather than pad along like this in the stupid expectation

23

of sensation. He further realised that he was himself now disliking the whole affair very much. Not that it didn't have one bright spot. Within a couple of minutes now, he was going to see the girl again.

'Can you tell me, Mr Appleby, for just how long you were in this vicinity before coming on the body?'

'Not more than ten minutes, I'd say. I drove up, got my clubs out of the car, walked to the first tee, got my drive well down the fairway, and landed my second in the bunker. And there the body was.'

'You didn't hear anything that might have been a shot? Or sounds of a quarrel, or a cry for help?'

'I didn't hear anything like any of these. As a matter of fact, I'm fairly sure the chap had been dead for some hours. I noticed—'

'Then it would be rather surprising, wouldn't it, if his murderers were only just making off, after enjoying a leisured roadside breakfast?'

'I never said—' Bobby checked himself. He remembered his father saying that Howard was a very sound man. And there was no point in getting annoyed. 'You'll judge for yourself,' he said. 'For here we are.'

They had rounded the spinney, and it was somehow with an effect of dramatic suddenness that the broad yellow bunker gaped before them. And Sergeant Howard's expectation of a reception committee was decidedly unfulfilled. There were no motorists. There was no girl. And there was no corpse. As in all the other bunkers on the course at this hour, the sand showed as neatly raked. Yet this one was not wholly like the others. For in the middle of it there still lay Bobby's ball. Sergeant Howard looked at it for a moment in silence—and so, for that matter, did the constable and the little group of goggling golfers. And then Howard spoke.

'Mr Appleby,' he said dispassionately, 'you seem to be in rather an awkward lie.'

CHAPTER TWO

'AWKWARD FOR THE boy.' Colonel Pride spoke sympatheti-
cally. When a friend's son gets into a scrape, it is best to
say little—but to say that little with decent warmth.
Tommy Pride, however, was obliged to say a good deal.
For he was the Chief Constable of the County, and when
it was John Appleby's boy who was in question he couldn't
do other than make the matter very much his own. And
there was more to it than Appleby's being a distinguished
colleague, now retired. The boy's mother was one of
Colonel Pride's oldest friends. He and Judith Raven had
been given their first ponies within a week of each other.
He had been right in the van of hopeful escorts in Judith's
first season. After that, of course, she had faded out of the
only sort of society that Tommy Pride knew. It was pre-
dictable, no doubt, since through some generations the
Ravens had tended to take up one or another activity of
the long-haired sort. And after that—for the Ravens were
freakish and unpredictable too—she had married her
policeman. Fortunately John Appleby, in addition to being
uncommonly able at his job, had proved to be a very
decent chap. And so too with the boy, Bobby. Rugger
Blue, capped for England, looked you straight in the eye.
A true-to-form Raven as well, however. Had written a book
for which Colonel Pride had dutifully paid thirty shillings.
Totally incomprehensible, but seemed to have been well-
received by people going in for that kind of thing. So this
affair on the golf-course was extremely vexatious. Colonel
Pride was quite annoyed about it.

'Damned stupid affair,' Colonel Pride said.

'Tommy—would you mind telling me frankly whether

anybody is saying that in the sense of insinuating that Bobby has cooked it all up?'

'Nobody's going to say that to *me*, John.' Colonel Pride, who was drinking Appleby's whisky in the library at Dream, set down his tumbler with an alarming crack on the marble chimney-piece. 'And Howard has no such idea in his head. It was plain to him from the start, he says, that Bobby believed his own story.' Pride paused. 'Of course there was the constable, who was with them when they walked up to this bunker. And there was the police surgeon, who arrived a minute or two later, and there were the ambulance men, who arrived a minute or two after that. There were some idlers as well—but they probably made nothing of it at all. You'll agree, I think, that it all adds up to something that can't exactly be kept quiet. That being so, we might as well run the perpetrators to earth, and have it in for them. Wouldn't you say?'

It was a moment before Appleby took in the implication of this. When he did so, he pushed his own tumbler away from him.

'Might as well?' he asked slowly. 'We might debate whether to or not? You take the whole thing to have been an idiotic joke—perpetrated not by Bobby, but upon him?'

'Howard is inclined to see it that way.' Colonel Pride reflected for a moment, and appeared to conclude that this was not quite a straight answer. 'I can't say more about myself, John, than that I'm at a good deal of a loss before the whole thing.'

'Bobby *felt* the body, you know. He got his hand on to the man's bare back. He says it was stone cold.'

'Howard maintains that any slightly chilly body will feel like that if you place a warm hand on it.'

'That is true. All the same, Tommy, any such theory positively posits my son as subject to hallucination. Think what he swears to—for it comes to that—about the state of the head.'

26

'Yes.' Colonel Pride looked unhappy. 'But there was no blood found in that confounded bunker—not even after they'd sifted down quite a way.'

'There needn't have been—if the man had been dead for some time before they chucked him there.'

'Howard says that.' Pride brightened a little at this. 'Only, you know, the whole thing is such nonsense. As a crime, I mean.'

'Tommy, are your people, or are they not, *treating* this as a crime?'

'Of course they are, so far as the most rigorous enquiry is concerned.' It looked for a moment as if Pride had been seriously offended. 'Owe it to your boy, my dear chap, to have every man in my force looking for a criminal. Nothing turned up yet. No line on a stranger to the district with a missing finger, or on an unknown girl, or on a car with two men and a trailer-caravan. And in point of what we can usefully look for, that's about it.'

'Certainly it is. Or that, and any report of a man gone missing elsewhere. A missing man with a missing finger—even if it were in Chicago or Marrakesh—would be a line at once.'

'Marrakesh?' For a moment Pride appeared to perpend this hyperbole conscientiously. 'Yes, of course. But we've had all that from your old colleagues at the Yard already. Remarkable efficiency nowadays in the way information is categorised. Several people with missing right forefingers have gone missing in the U.K. in the last ten years. But, dead or alive, all have turned up again. So that tells us nothing at all.'

'In a fairly short time, Tommy, it might tell us quite a lot. If you grant that there *was* a body—and an entirely dead one—then the fact that nobody in the near future starts enquiring about a missing man mutilated in this way—'

'That would put the corpse roughly in a category, I agree.

What they call a drop-out, or the like. Incidentally, your son says the fellow's clothes suggested reasonable prosperity.' Pride hesitated. 'Do you know? I gather Bobby won't say much about the girl. She was blonde and a lady. He doesn't go much beyond that.'

'Gentlemen prefer blondes.'

'Just what do you mean by that?'

'Not a great deal, perhaps.' Appleby hesitated. The affair of the body in the bunker was, in an important sense, very much Bobby's own affair. He mustn't be nudged by his father unless he asked to be nudged. He mustn't even be too much talked about, even to a family friend like Tommy Pride. On the other hand, something patent about Bobby that Pride or Pride's men simply hadn't noticed might just as well be named now. 'Only,' Appleby said, 'that the boy seems to have been rather struck by the girl.'

Pride drained his whisky, and shook his head as Appleby's hand went hospitably out to the decanter. He gave a moment to examining the empty fireplace, and a couple more to finding and lighting a cigarette. It was clear that the admirable man felt this whole damnable piece of jiggery-pokery to have its delicate side.

'Easy on the eyes, and all that?' he asked. 'Clean-cut girl? I'm sure your boy would have good taste where a filly's concerned. But you don't think he's sitting tight on something because of having taken a fancy to her? Chivalry—that sort of thing?'

Appleby's amusement at this string of questions didn't prevent his taking a moment or two to reflect in his turn.

'It's hard to say, Tommy. Perhaps it depends on how your chap Howard—for whom I've a high regard—has been viewing the girl. Is it as an accomplice of the villains, supposing there to have been a crime—or of the jokers, on the weird theory that Bobby was being taken in by a piece of macabre fun? Or does he suppose the girl to have been a victim, just as Bobby was?'

'I think Howard supposes the girl to have been—well, not on Bobby's side. And it's difficult, you know, to view it in any other way. After all, she had cleared out—along with the body, if it was a body, and the chaps in the car, granting that they had anything to do with the affair. Otherwise, why didn't she stay put, or run for the club-house, or just give a shout? A good loud halloo would have carried that far, I'd say.' Yet again, Pride hesitated. 'I know that Bobby behaved perfectly correctly to my people. But I rather wish he was still here now. You and I could have had another quiet word with the boy, eh? As it is, the brute fact seems to be that he vanished from Dream early this afternoon.'

'Am I to understand that Howard asked him to remain for the time being at Dream?'

'Nothing of the kind.' Colonel Pride had hastily shaken his head. 'Boy has been perfectly correct, as I say.'

'My dear Tommy, we'd better get this clear. If Bobby formed a notion as to what was in Howard's head—the notion that he had been taken in by a gruesome and pointless practical joke—then the boy had a perfect right to take a certain measure of offence. Or call it umbrage, if you prefer the word.'

'I quite see—'

'And please consider this.' For the first time, Appleby's voice had gone a shade grim. 'He's still very young. And—whether for good or ill—he's been given fair ground for considering himself quite other than a fool—'

'My dear fellow!' The Chief Constable's discomfort was now acute. 'Absolutely brilliant, of course. We all know it. There never was a Raven who was all bone above the neck.' Pride positively floundered—glimpsing, perhaps, a certain lack of the felicitous in thus instantly directing his thought to the Raven side of the house. 'I quite see what you mean.'

'I don't know that you do.' For the moment, Appleby's astringency didn't relax. 'There's another very possible reason why this girl may, as you express it, have cleared out. She may have been cleared out—say at the point of a gun. A man needn't have taken a First in Greats, or even have written an anti-novel or whatever it's called, to tumble to that. Now, if Bobby sees the thing that way—persons unknown making off, for some mysterious reason, with a murdered man and a living girl—what is he likely to do?'

'Go after them, I suppose.'

'It's a fair enough bet.' Appleby's asperity vanished. 'By the way, do you happen to know whether he told Howard of any notion he had about the dead man's possible identity?'

'I don't think Bobby came forward with anything of that kind.'

'Um.' For the first time, Appleby confessed to himself an uneasy sense that Bobby had perhaps gone hazardously out on a limb.

'I believe he said he'd once known a man with a missing index-finger. But you can't mean that. Howard took it for rather a trivial remark.'

Appleby checked an impulse to say 'Um' again. He wasn't sure that he wouldn't have to revise his opinion of Howard.

'You mean,' he asked, 'that Howard brushed the information aside?'

'My dear John, I don't know that that's altogether fair. If you think there could be anything in it, you must have a word with Howard yourself. And it can be taken up again as soon as Bobby gets home.'

'Perfectly true.' Appleby again reminded himself that he wasn't playing Bobby's hand for him. It was, of course, extremely serious to withhold a scrap of information from the police—even from a policeman convinced that one had been made some sort of ass of. But this didn't mean that Appleby himself need start talking about an obscure schoolmaster called Nauze here and now. 'Wherever

Bobby's gone off to,' he said pacifically, 'I expect he'll ring up this evening. I'll let you know at once if he has anything sensible to say.'

But Bobby didn't ring up—or not by eleven o'clock, the hour after which the senior Applebys discouraged telephone-calls from their children. Appleby was far from alarmed. He had very little doubt where Bobby had gone off to, since there was only one spot in England in which he had any immediate prospect of picking up a trail on the man who used to be called Bloody Nauze. And at least at his old private school Bobby was more likely to pick up something useful about the man than would be an officer from a C.I.D. Old hands at Overcombe would be prepared to gossip with Bobby (a distinguished Old Boy) as they would not be with a policeman.

Appleby was restless, all the same. He wished that his wife hadn't gone off on one of her London jaunts. In Judith's absence—and Bobby's—the establishment at Dream was a little lacking in intellectual calibre. Mrs Colpoys in the kitchen had her heart in the right place, and expressed extreme indignation at Mr Robert's having had his early-morning golf interrupted in that nasty way. She thought it likely that the dead man had fallen out of an aeroplane—probably a helicopter, which had then descended and picked him up again. She believed that people fell out of such contraptions far more frequently than was known. It was the sort of thing the authorities kept quiet about.

Out in the garden the aged Hoobin, pausing in his day's work (which chiefly consisted in issuing directions to his nephew and assistant young Solo Hoobin), had offered a number of remarks too gnomic in manner to be very certainly understood, but having apparent relevance to the darkest recesses of sexual crime. The aged Hoobin was the owner of a pair of spectacles (which had been given him by old Lady Killcanon along with a copy of the Bible) and had as a consequence set himself up in the dignity of what he called a perusing man. He still read the Bible on week-days, but on Sundays he read *The News of the World*. He thus achieved, no doubt, a balanced view of the whole nature of man. Yet temperamentally he inclined increasingly to a sombre interpretation of human character and motive. Moreover, he had lately been taking bold steps in the exploration of morbid psychology.

'There be them,' Hoobin had said to his employer, 'who be one man today and another man tomorrow. And there be them that be one man this hour and another man that hour. So it do be said to be.'

'Would you say it was true of everybody?' Appleby asked. It was his intention to suggest that while Solo put sickle to one verge of the drive Hoobin himself might put sickle to the other. But the best chance of achieving this lay in first giving Hoobin his head as a sage. 'Would you say'—he achieved a great effect of sharpening a philosophical discussion—'it was true of Solo?'

Solo began whistling defiantly. He always did this when he heard his name mentioned.

'Solo be nothing of a man.' Hoobin would have made an excellent performer in a mediaeval disputation; he was a master of the *distinguo*. 'Not yet wench-high, Solo be. And all childer be unaccountable quite.'

Solo suddenly fell to whetting his sickle with demoniacal vigour. Appleby wondered if he were indulging some monstrous fantasy of eviscerating his aged uncle.

'But Mr Robert,' Hoobin pursued, ''a bin wench-high and over them three years and more. The vittels ha the doing on't. High living in the colleges. That and being flown with wine.'

'Mr Robert,' Appleby said with some severity, 'is a very temperate young man.'

'He be that when he be one man.' Hoobin pounced on

the thread of his former argument. 'But what when he be another? And they do disremember, the one does, what t'other done. The right hand, Sir John, knowth not what the left hand doth. So the scholards ha brought it out.'

Solo—who was a perfect natural only at the full of the moon—had stopped whistling, and was blunting the point of his sickle by doodling with it in the gravel of the drive. A sideways glance revealed to Appleby the rudiments of a squat and boldly callipygian female form. Prehistoric Man had been a dab-hand at this in leisure moments devoted to meditations upon fertility. Some deep atavism was prompting Solo to this means of asserting that his uncle's estimate of his imperfect maturity was fallacious. Appleby reflected, as he had frequently had occasion to do before, that the Hoobins were a tribe who should be living not in council cottages but in caves. The thought resulted in his losing for a moment the drift of Hoobin's remarks.

'And it be the word at the Killcanon Arms,' Hoobin was saying, 'that her corpus be not found yet.'

'*His* corpus, you mean?'

'That her corpus be not found yet. But time uncovers all. First a leg 'twill be, and then an arm. Let them look in the railway station, I say, where folk leave their trunks and parcels.'

Appleby parted from the Hoobins with some abruptness—leaving Hoobin to return, unperturbed, to telling Solo what to do. It was evident that quite a lot was abroad about the trio who had met at the bunker. And Bobby was being cast hopefully in the role of some fiendish Jekyll and Hyde. Judith wouldn't have turned a hair at this manifestation of the rustic mind, but it at least had power to return several times to Appleby's thoughts during a solitary evening. At half-past eleven and with a second cigar (which was a sign of disquiet in itself) he went out into the garden.

*   *   *

33

There was a tremendous moon—so that he almost expected to encounter Solo offering conjurations to it. The ancient house was laved in its light, like some creature of stone over which the waters of a gentle fountain flow down on every flank. The lawn was a sheet of silver—like water too, but of an utter stillness, so that one could have imagined some craft of obtrusively poetic character—say an elfin pinnace—to come gliding over it at any moment. The acacia tree was a scented cascade, and a nightingale was singing amid its long racemes. All the works, Appleby told himself. Absolutely all the works.

But the garden failed to hold him, and when he had prowled round the house he found that he had halted before the motor-sheds. This cleared his mind for him. He got out the car, and drove over to Linger.

There was nothing on the road except a hedgehog, a hare; and his mind could play as it pleased. When Bobby was at home, how regularly did he go out before breakfast and play a few holes? Perhaps, Appleby told himself, two or three times a week. Which wasn't enough for his turning up to be gambled on. So the body hadn't been disposed in its bunker for Bobby's specific benefit. Or not unless one imagined a scout with an eye on Dream, and a swift telephone-message as soon as Bobby set out. But nothing of the sort would allow much time to fix up an elaborate piece of miching malicho. That it was Bobby who had come upon the body appeared, therefore, almost certainly fortuitous.

But *somebody* had been expected to come upon it. Either some other specific somebody, or whoever among the morning's golfers first propelled his ball in the direction of the first green. You don't choose the fairway of a golf-course if you are anxious to keep a dead man concealed for any length of time. Of course you may simply shoot a man down where he happens to be, and abandon him on the spot—or near the spot—in a panic. In that case, it

34

isn't relevant to speak of expectations at all.

But if the dead man, already dead, had been transported quite some way, then there must at least have been a reason—although possibly a muddled or feeble one—for dumping him just where he had been dumped. But then he had been up-lifted again! This was the point of real astonishment—and one which surely counted against the notion of a muddled or feeble job. For whatever reason it had been done, nerve had been required for the doing. And think of the raking over of the sand, and the leaving of Bobby's ball in the middle of it. More nerve had been required for that—and perhaps a grim sort of humour as well. It might have been calculated, of course, that Bobby's story would be totally discredited; that without further inquiry the police would dismiss the whole thing. Tommy Pride had revealed, indeed, that it had almost come to that. But nobody could really have banked on it. Even if it had been the sole motive in raking over the surface of the bunker, it could hardly have been the sole motive for carrying off the body.

Why exhibit a dead man, and then spirit him away again? There existed, no doubt, conceivable answers to this question. But Appleby couldn't at the moment supply one, so he had to ask himself another question instead. What could precipitate a hazardous change of plan? Abandoning a murdered man on a golf-course was not in itself remarkable. It didn't, so to speak, cry out for explanation. But whipping the murdered man away again did. And for this—at least in general terms—an explanation could be given. Something had gone wrong. There had been a hitch.

And the hitch had been either Bobby or the girl.

These thoughts brought Appleby to the club-house. As he walked up to it from his parked car his footfalls, first on macadam and then on gravel, sounded loud to his own ear. But nobody was going to detect him on this nocturnal expedition. There were no living-quarters, he remembered, in the club-house, and it seemed unlikely that anybody would have thought up the ploy of playing golf by moonlight. The course, it was true, was by no means remote from human habitation. On this side it was bounded for nearly half a mile by a high-road—the high-road upon which Bobby and the girl had remarked a car, a trailer, and two men. And some fifty yards back from the other verge of this ran a straggle of substantial villas—mostly the homes, Appleby supposed, of retired persons who prized the contiguity of a golf-course beyond all else, and who when not playing themselves liked to survey from their drawing-room windows other people doing so. In a way, therefore, this part of the course was likely to be under scrutiny at any daylight hour—or any moonlight hour, for that matter, by somebody of wakeful habit. Yet the whole terrain had one marked peculiarity. There was a great deal of timber on it—far more than would be acceptable on a fashionable modern course, so that one was regularly banging one's ball down what were in effect very broad avenues, or skying it over hazel copses, or agonisingly writhing one's own body in the hope of magically deflecting it from large patches of gorse.

It would all have been rather good ground for hide-and-seek of the outdoor variety. Or it would serve for those primitive war-games which Bobby had appeared to enjoy as a schoolboy in his O.T.C. You had a section or (if you were grand) a platoon, and you had quite a lot of blank cartridges, and you were told that there was an enemy machine-gun in this position or that, and that you had to work out how to capture it without losing quite all your men. And indeed in these broad moonlit spaces and dark enfilading woods and sudden impassable thickets it was perfectly possible to imagine much more sinister carryings-on than that. Or at least it was possible to do so under Solo

Hoobin's luminary. By daylight any golf-course is a place banal enough.

The hitch had been either Bobby or the girl. Counting his paces from the club-house to the first green, Appleby repeated this conviction. He did so by way of reminding himself that he mustn't jump to the conclusion that the hitch had assuredly been Bobby. Bobby had said something to the girl suggesting that the corpse might be known to him, and it was after this that the corpse had vanished. The inference seemed as open as a Dutch barn. The girl had got Bobby off the scene, had alerted confederates to an unexpected danger, and they had made off, dead body and all—and after putting on that turn in the bunker with a rake. The body, in fact, had been brought from some remote place. It had been dumped where it was overwhelmingly improbable that it would ever be identified. Then Bobby had come along, had noticed the missing index-finger, had divulged to the girl—

Appleby broke off this train of speculation. In one aspect it seemed almost too easy. In another, there were things it just didn't start to explain. So it might be radically wrong. For example, it might get the girl—the totally unaccountable girl—quite on the wrong side of the fence. She might be totally unconnected with the crime; might be no more than an innocent early-morning stroller over the golf-course. That, after all, was clearly how Bobby had seen her. When Bobby had made for the club-house and the telephone, she had made for the road and the two men with the caravan and the car. It had been her business to make them stay put until the police arrived, so that it might be discovered whether they had anything useful to tell. Mightn't she, tumbling out her story, have explained that there was a young man who thought he was possibly in a position to identify the corpse? And mightn't the men be in fact the murderers—for it seemed impossible that anything short of murder could be in question—and might not the issue be that, in deciding they must take the body elsewhere, they decided that the girl was too dangerous to leave behind? That was almost certainly what Bobby had decided. And the further possibilities seemed very grim. By this time there might be two corpses instead of one— and the second would be a wholly innocent girl's.

Appleby walked on to the first green, or rather to the fatal bunker guarding it. He walked by the direct route, which was straight through the little spinney. That was how a voice would travel. One had to reckon, of course, that the screen of trees would exercise a certain blanketing effect. Even so, on a still morning and with no distracting noise coming from the high-road, a woman's voice raised full-pitch here by the bunker ought to be audible at the club-house. But not, perhaps, to a young man preoccupied with making a telephone-call. Coming to a halt on the lip of the bunker, Appleby shook his head over this unresolvable point. If his nocturnal jaunt was not to be merely fruitless, he must find some other aspect of the affair which might yield something to reconnaissance.

Bobby had said the body was quite cold, and its clothes wet with dew, when he came upon it. At a rough guess, therefore, the man had been dead round about midnight, and exposed to the air through the small hours. But of course he hadn't necessarily been thus exposed in the bunker. He might have been flung in there only shortly before Bobby turned up. And the police had found no traces of blood. Given the very short space of time available to whoever had carried the body off again, it thus seemed doubtful that it had been in the bunker that the man was killed. So why had he been dumped in it at all? Could it be in order to *time*—if only approximately—the hour at which it was likely to be found?

Here you are—Appleby told himself as he surveyed the moon-blanched scene—with a corpse on a golf-course. With a corpse on *this* golf-course. What do you do if you want its discovery delayed for rather a long time? You give yourself (or, more probably, your several selves) an uncomfortable ten minutes getting it more or less into the heart of one of those big gorse thickets—where it will perhaps be months until some player penetrates to it while hunting, with quite exceptional pertinacity, for a lost ball. What do you do if you want it never to be found at all? You go to the great labour of getting it well underground and then obliterating the traces of your grave-digging. What if you don't care *when* it's found? You simply leave it where, conceivably, it is—bang in the middle of one of these fairways. But at this end of the course this means on terrain largely commanded from the high-road; and in bright moonlight your body might be spotted from the first passing car. All right, if you don't care a bit. But suppose you want *some* time to elapse—enough, say, for a good get-away—but that the body should *certainly* be found soon after that? You shove it in the bunker. It is invisible from the road. But, next day, the first man to play the first hole will come upon it.

Appleby wondered whether he would be better in bed. Reasoning like this was sound enough in itself, but all it led to was another conundrum. Why, with a murdered man on his hands, should anybody want to make sure of that murdered man's being stumbled upon in anything between, say, six and nine hours' time? It wasn't the sort of question to which Appleby's professional experience was at all likely to find him stumped for an answer—*some* answer. It might, for example, be desirable to have witnesses to the fact of death having occurred before a certain bank opened on a certain morning. Again, although a good part of the man's head had—according to Bobby—been shot or similarly blasted away, the dead man might actually have been poisoned. There are poisons which break up even in a dead organism, and are thus not detectable after a time. The people who had chosen the bunker for their corpse had been minded to ensure the successful *post-mortem* detection of something of the sort. Or yet again—

Appleby broke off from these hopeful reflections. He had been continuing to gaze at the bunker. His own shadow cut across it laterally—a shadow as hard as clear sunlight would cast, and showing like a chasm between two surfaces which sparkled and glittered like finely powdered glass. And suddenly the chasm had widened as if the impulsion of some small seismic disturbance—or as if Appleby (the sole cause of its existence, after all) were in some frog-like way monstrously distending himself. A moment later this figure of unnatural girth had split in two. Appleby's shadow lay distinguishably across the bunker once more. And so did the shadow of another man.

Appleby swung swiftly round—much as Bobby, from a similar stance, had done before him. Appleby was perhaps more alarmed than Bobby had been; he had known some very tight corners leap into being rather in this fashion. But at least the man now behind him was making no move to bash him on the head. The man's hands, indeed, were both in the pockets of a light overcoat—which was a garment not really needed on so mild a night. Nor did the man much require a Homburg hat—but a Homburg hat he had, tilted well down over the eyes. These facts, and the further fact of his standing, relatively to Appleby, in sharp silhouette, did produce something conceivably to be termed sinister in effect. Certainly they rendered the man momentarily unidentifiable, so that he had spoken before Appleby could put a name to him.

'Good evening, Sir John,' Sergeant Howard said.

The moment was faintly awkward, although it was not quite clear why it need be. The hour was now late. Or rather it was very early, since it was substantially past midnight. Appleby's presence on the golf-course was perhaps odd. But Howard's, after all, was a good deal odder. Appleby decided to begin by making this point.

'Good evening, Sergeant. This affair must be as much on your mind as on mine.'

'Properly so, I hope.'

'Well, yes.' Appleby was checked momentarily by the stiffness of this. 'But it's simply the day's work with you—whereas, on any reading of the thing, it's my own son who has had a fairly shocking experience on this golf-course. So I'm surprised to find it haunting *you* in the small hours. Particularly as I gather you feel it may all have been a joke.'

'I'm not *treating* it as a joke, sir.' Howard produced this soberly. 'That's just one possible interpretation.'

'You seem to have stressed it to the Chief Constable.'

'True enough. But it won't do any harm—wouldn't you agree?—if Colonel Pride, who is a communicative gentleman, airs that notion here and there.'

'Well, I'm blessed!' Appleby was astonished, but not unattracted, by this bold manner of regarding a superior. 'You mean to say you're actually concerned to have it get around that the police are inclined to regard the thing as a prank either by my son or by somebody else?'

'Something of the kind, Sir John—although I'm speaking of what is past history now, as I'll explain in a moment. I've felt, if I may say so, what may be called an upper-class slant to this mystery. I don't see that girl, for instance, as only casually connected with it, and she seems to have been out of that drawer, if your son is to be believed. Very well. It struck me that there might be somebody with his ear to the ground somewhere in the society Colonel Pride frequents. It might be useful to circulate at least a persuasion that we have been taken in more or less as we were plainly meant to be taken in. That we are *not* hot-foot after murder.'

'But we are?' It was with increased astonishment that

Appleby employed the drenching moonlight to scrutinise more closely the expression of this unusual police sergeant. 'You haven't a doubt of it?'

'It stands to reason, doesn't it?' There was a frankly reproachful note in Howard's voice. 'Of course, I told your son he had landed himself with something uncommonly awkward. That was only fair. But I think I'm correct in believing his head to be screwed on the right way?'

'I'm not an impartial witness, Sergeant. But you're probably not far wrong.'

'And he has eyes in it, for that matter. So we know what we're facing, clearly enough. But why let on that we do? That's why I persuaded the Chief Constable to let me try to keep it out of the press, and just have a bit of rumour going around. To repeat, sir: the people who killed the unknown man were careful to leave *this*'—Howard gestured towards the bunker—'neat and tidy—as one might hope to find it, you might say. They did so in the hope that your son's story would be discounted. Don't let's disabuse them yet. That was the line I worked on. Only this afternoon, sir, it went wrong. And it went wrong because I slipped up badly.'

'I'm surprised to hear it,' Appleby said quietly.

'There was a telephone-call from the Home Office. They wanted information.'

'The Home Office?' Appleby was puzzled. 'But you'd been getting data from Missing Persons at Scotland Yard, hadn't you? Why on earth should the Home Office—'

'Yes, Sir John. But I didn't work out that one until five minutes too late. It was a Principal. He gave his name, and sounded uncommonly steamed up. He said there had been a gross irregularity of procedure, and that the Minister himself was gravely concerned.'

'The Home Secretary gravely concerned about this! My dear man—'

'Yes, sir. But you must remember that I don't have your

familiarity with Whitehall. And all he wanted was confirmation that we had good reason to believe there had been the body of a dead man with a missing finger discovered on this golf course during the early morning of—'

'I see. So you confirmed it—and then began to wonder? And your wondering took just five minutes?'

'Just about that. So I called back the Home Office—which took a bit of nerve, Sir John, as you will understand—and nobody knew what I was talking about. They weren't too pleased at being bothered by a rural policeman who'd plainly been taken in by some joker in a callbox.'

'Too bad, Sergeant.' Appleby laughed in rather a muted way. Standing just where he did, he had an irrational sense of being in the presence of the dead. 'But I've been taken in often enough in rather the same fashion, I must confess.'

'Well, there's consolation in that.' Howard paused on what was his own first ray of humour. 'But something further followed. One of my men brought me the midday edition of one of the evening papers. Somewhere or other, there's been a leak. It carried a fairly full account of your son's adventure. But perhaps you've seen it?'

'We don't take an evening paper.' Appleby thought for a moment. 'You think the telephone-call was precipitated by the newspaper report? It was an attempt to get official police confirmation of what the paper might, or might not, have got accurately?'

'It looks that way to me.'

'Tell me, Sergeant—is the newspaper precise about the time of the discovery?'

'No, sir.'

'But the fellow on the telephone got that out of you?'

'Certainly he did. And I'm bound to say I feel a fool. It's not how one wants to feel, when an affair of this sort comes one's way. It's an uncommon chance—here in a country situation.'

'Perfectly true, Sergeant.' Appleby was interested in this frank avowal on Howard's part of some touch of the last infirmity of noble mind. 'But it's early days yet. And at least you know more than you knew this morning.'

'Yes, sir. I know there are other sleuths on the trail.'

'Meaning my son and myself?'

'Not that, at all.' This time, Howard managed a subdued laugh himself. 'I don't fancy it was an Appleby who was on the other end of that telephone-line.'

'In that case, Sergeant, may I ask just what is your present reading of the affair?'

'Well, Sir John, since you ask, I'll offer a guess. We're far from being up against a one-man show. There's quite a little crowd of villains somewhere. And they're not trusting one another very far.'

Part Two

DR GULLIVER'S SCHOOL

CHAPTER THREE

OVERCOMBE DIDN'T SEEM to have changed much. Nor did
Dr Gulliver. A dozen years ago the black stuff gown per-
petually worn by Dr Gulliver was green with age, and it
was green with age still. Only, Bobby was now able to
identify it as an Oxford M.A. gown. He wondered—as he
had certainly never done as a small boy—whether Dr
Gulliver was really a Doctor of anything, or whether, as
a headmaster, he was 'Doctor' merely in a courtesy or
Dickensian sense. It had always been understood, of
course, that Dr Gulliver was immensely learned. It was on
this that he had, so to speak, run; and it had never occurred
to anybody to reflect that unfathomable erudition is
neither necessary nor customary in the proprietor—or co-
proprietor—of a private school.

It had sometimes come to Bobby to wonder why on earth
he had been sent to Overcombe; or how, once there, he
had ever managed to progress, through a respectable showing in Common Entrance, to a decent public school. Perhaps the flair of Bloody Nauze for driving home the Latin
language with a gym-shoe was the answer. Not that there
had been anything much wrong with Overcombe, apart
from the mere fact that a species of total chaos reigned
there from the beginning of term to the end. It had probably been different in the days of his mother's great-uncles.
They had been to Overcombe, and had all become lumin-
aries of the Victorian Age. *That*, no doubt, was why Bobby
had arrived there what he thought of as about a century
later. That was how parents chose schools for children.
They didn't specifically hunt around for an establishment
where there were people like Dr Gulliver and Mr Onslow

and Mr Nauze; they just recalled how happy some aged relation of their own had been rumoured to be at Overcombe or whatever.

'Appleby?' Dr Gulliver. '*Appleby?*' Dr Gulliver twitched his gown—and with his old nervous haste, so that it was incomprehensible that the decayed garment didn't at once disintegrate under his finger and thumb. 'But—to be sure —Appleby! You made some slight progress in the end towards a grasp of the Punic Wars. I trust, Appleby, that you still keep to your book.'

The Punic Wars. *The Pubic Wars.* Bobby had been among the small number of precocious infants at Overcombe who could make jokes like that. The ability was gained through the pertinacious frequentation of a dictionary. *Womb, Concubine, Harlot, Semen.* Briefly, Bobby marvelled over his own dead life.

'Are you still in partnership with Mr Onslow, sir?' Bobby asked respectfully.

'Ah—F. L.! Onslow is always called F.L. by the young rascals. Do you know what the initials F.L. stand for?'

'I've no idea, I'm afraid.'

'The jest must have been invented since your time. *Festina lente*, Appleby. It is the motto of Mr Onslow's— um—somewhat remote kinsmen. Construe, my dear lad.'

'Would it be something like "More haste, less speed", sir?'

'A most licentious translation.' Dr Gulliver had frowned majestically. 'We will say, if you please, "Hasten slowly".'

'I see, sir. It's a terribly good joke. Mr Onslow being F.L., I mean.'

'Onslow is still with us, I am happy to say. The—um— athletic side continues in his charge, and we must not minimise its importance. *Mens sana*, Appleby, *in corpore sano.*'

'Is that Latin, sir?' Entirely to his own horror, the obligation to 'cheek' Dr Gulliver had reared itself suddenly and irresistibly out of Bobby's past.

'It is a sufficiently well-known apothegm, I should have supposed.' Dr Gulliver had frowned in displeasure. 'Though not, indeed, from an author who is to be commended to the young. The aphorism comes from Juvenal's Tenth Satire.'

'By Jove, sir—so it does. *Fortem posce animum mortis terrore carentem*—would that be right?—*Qui spatium vitae extremum inter munera ponat Naturae*—' Bobby broke off, not because he had forgotten Juvenal's prayer, but because he remembered he hadn't come back to Overcombe as an undergraduate lark. 'I'll be tremendously interested to meet Mr Onslow again,' he said. 'And any other of the masters in my time who are still here.'

This cautious approach to the topic of Mr Nauze yielded no immediate result. Dr Gulliver had jumped to his feet with what Bobby now vividly remembered as his chronic senseless agitation. It was this—or rather it was the schizoid pairing of this with his answering air of a scholar's deeply meditative habit—that gave Dr Gulliver his peculiarly bizarre note. Indeed (Bobby now saw), it was doubtless from this nervous peculiarity of the Doctor that Overcombe as a school derived its special quality of craziness. The thing didn't, so far as his recollection went, at all disturb the pupils. Almost all small boys are mad; the really terrifying aspect of graduating to a public school at twelve or thirteen was the abrupt demand the transition made for an assumption of the appearances of sanity. It was at about thirteen (Mr Robert Appleby, brilliantly paradoxical novelist, reflected) that the individual is condemned to enter what the poet Yeats calls the stupidity of one's middle years.

'You must see the extensions and improvements,' Dr Gulliver was saying. 'We owe them to the piety—I use the word in its classical sense of *pietas*, Appleby—of our old boys. Of *many* of our old boys.' Dr Gulliver favoured

Bobby with a penetrating glare. 'But there has been a marked short-fall, I am sorry to say, upon the total sum required. It looks as if the swimming-pool, for example, is to land us in a state of liquidation.' Dr Gulliver paused —perhaps as a profound philologist aware that he had struck out a notably complex image. 'Not all of my former charges, I am sorry to say, have come forward to suckle their *alma mater*.' Dr Gulliver made a longer pause. Perhaps he was sorting this one out in his head. Not that he hadn't aimed a shaft at Bobby accurately enough.

'I'm afraid I didn't hear about a subscription,' Bobby said unblushingly. 'I've been in Samarkand.'

'Indeed? Well, boys will be boys—and run into trouble from time to time. Be assured, Appleby, that your old school thinks none the worse of you.' Dr Gulliver, who had been making for the door of his study, had stopped in his tracks. Bobby wondered whether he could conceivably be suffering from some rare disorder of the auditory system which tended to bring out 'Samarkand' as 'Sing Sing' or 'Wormwood Scrubs' or 'Pentonville'. But now Dr Gulliver was speaking again. 'I have no doubt,' he was asking, 'that you carry your cheque-book with you?'

Bobby—who was very much in earnest about his visit to Overcombe—acknowledged the inescapable, and paid up.

They wandered about the large disfurnished mansion. Dr Gulliver's extensions and improvements, if they really existed, seemed not of an obtrusive order. The form-rooms were quite unchanged—except that their bare wooden floors had been scrubbed into yet deeper grooves under the exertions of the luckless old women from the village who came in to do that sort of thing. There were the same photographs of classical statuary on the walls—revoltingly naked and resoundingly anaphrodisiac, as if purveyed by some firm of scholastic suppliers expert in sustaining the moral probity of the young. The ancient desks, plainly designed to be bolted to the floor in orderly rows, stood around in a random way like guests at a disordered party. Pen-knives had not ceased to be at work on them; Bobby particularly admired one inscription so precisely cut as clearly to represent the full-time labour of a term; it said YOGI BEAR WAS HEAR. Another, more rapidly executed, said BAWLS TO FATGUTS GULLIVER. Yet another appeared to be the despairing prayer of a learned child, since it read ORARE POTTER MINOR. Just as long ago, not much appeared to be done in the way of tidying up. Football-boots smothered in dried clay lay where they had been kicked into corners a term ago, their long, muddied laces writhing around them. Stamp-albums; primitive musical instruments; desiccated goldfish in abandoned bowls; rejected pin-ups of male persons celebrated in one or another athletic world; the crumpled wrappings of Munchies, Crunchies, Scrumpties, Mintoes, Chockoes, Maltoes and the like; boring letters from aunts; mildly miniaturised tennis-rackets and cricket-bats: all these silted up the interstices of these chambers devoted to the pursuit of learning. As he surveyed them, Bobby felt himself assailed by an unwholesome nostalgia. It was as if he sighed for garments too short in the arm and leg, for ink on his fingers and revolting hair-creams experimentally applied to his scalp. He had to recall himself abruptly to a present world in which one or two nasty things had taken place.

Bobby's chief problem was the girl. Objectively and subjectively, she was very much a puzzle. What had happened to her? Anybody—any responsible person—would have to be interested in that. She had vanished while hard up against some brutal crime, and in circumstances which remained wholly mysterious. That was the external enigma. But there was a further enigma inside Bobby's head. Was he more involved in tracing her—or in rescuing her, as it must surely be—than if she were just *any* young woman similarly circumstanced? It had been for only three or four minutes that she had existed for him. And she had existed only as a voice, a figure in the fragrance of dawn. That sort of thing is something you lay on when going after effects of cheap romance. So perhaps he had involved himself in a foolish entanglement of that sort.

Bobby had given a great deal of thought to sex, and had concluded, on grounds of high theory, that the individual's approach to it ought to be variously experimental. Unfortunately he could hardly recall an occasion upon which he himself had contrived to experiment with sex, since sex always seemed to get ahead and experiment with him. Perhaps that was what was happening again now. It was undeniable that he knew hardly anything whatever about this girl—not even whether she had an interesting mind or a nice smell. Yet here he was—plainly on the verge of losing sleep over her in the very largest way.

He recalled himself to his surroundings in Overcombe School. This business of pottering round with Gulliver was of no use whatever. He simply wanted to find out from Gulliver—or, if not from Gulliver himself, then from some other old inhabitant—what had happened to a former assistant master called Nauze. It was possible that nobody would remember anything about him. He might hardly have impressed himself on his colleagues at all. With *them*, he hadn't enjoyed the freedom of a gym shoe for that purpose. On the other hand, somebody just *might* turn up with a handful of information which would either exclude or make slightly less arbitrary the strange possibility Bobby had thought up about the identity of the body in the bunker.

They passed through a day-room deserted except for two small boys absorbed in a game of chess. With automatic omniscience, Dr Gulliver paused to direct one of them in the move he should next make. In another room quite a little crowd were quarrelling over the running of a model railway. Yet a third, however, afforded a glimpse of some dozen studious infants sitting in well ordered rows while producing with a weary docility the animal-like noises which in an English school pass for the language of Racine and Voltaire. The time-table at Overcombe had always been like that. Sometimes a single lesson would go on bewilderingly for hours, while at other times almost the entire staff vanished for days on end. And Bloody Nauze, come to think of it, had done rather more vanishing than most.

'Can you tell me,' Bobby asked, 'what happened to Mr Nauze?'

'And now we must visit the playing-fields.' Dr Gulliver, who had halted very abruptly in his tracks, made one of his sub-phrenetic dashes towards an outer door. For a moment Bobby had a hopeful feeling that his question, thus obtrusively ignored, had at least for some mysterious reason been a disconcerting one. But perhaps nothing more had been involved than Gulliver's general battiness. And now they were traversing a large derelict conservatory (described in the prospectus of Overcombe as 'affording abundant opportunity for simple horticultural experiments') on their way to the open air. 'For our annual Sports approach,' the Doctor was saying. 'The prizes, I am delighted to be able to divulge, will be presented by Air-Vice-Marshal Synn-Essery. Synn-Essery—the family, as you know, is of the highest antiquity—is not among the least distinguished of Overcombe's *alumni*. Mr Onslow—whose people, by the way, hold some kinship with the Synn-Esserys—is naturally concerned that everything should go with even more than the customary éclat. We shall find him, I think, superintending the construction of the Long Jump.'

This proved to be true. Mr Onslow—so wittily nick-named F.L.—was giving instruction to a number of the young gentlemen of Overcombe in the art of cutting turfs and shovelling sand. (The prospectus called this 'encouragement to learn something of the rural skills and crafts with which the simplest country gentleman should be familiar'.) Unlike Dr Gulliver, Mr Onslow had changed a good deal. He had changed, in fact, by several stone. He had also changed in complexion. Above the enormous pink Leander scarf which (surprisingly, on a warm summer day) was swathed several times round his neck, the face of Mr Onslow showed as a discordant beetroot. Probably he was being further throttled by the flaunting red, yellow and black of his I Zingari tie. His blazer, which asserted to the initiate that he had rowed for Cambridge in some year unknown, was no longer adequate to his girth. This, however, helped further to broadcast the notable catholicity of Mr Onslow's athletic achievements, since what the gap revealed was a sweater proper to be worn by those who have played Association Football for Oxford. It was impossible to conceive that the motto *festina lente* had been much attended to by this universally accomplished person in his younger days.

'Ah, Onslow,' Dr Gulliver said. 'You will remember—um—Appleby.'

'No.' It was with conviction, and after only the briefest glance at Bobby, that Mr Onslow responded with this monosyllable. 'Beadon, you young lout, look nippy with that barrow, or I'll have the skin off you.'

'Vellee-vellee good, sahib.' Beadon, a slender and fair child whom Dr Gulliver would have been able to authenticate to the gratified enquirer as one of the Wiltshire Beadons, was not perturbed. And Bobby, glancing at Onslow, recalled that this stupid, boorish and unquestionably spurious athlete had never been known to apply any instrument of correction, whether licensed or unlicensed, to the person of any of his charges. It seemed a considerable virtue to Bobby, and for a moment he found himself wishing that Onslow didn't dislike him to the extent he

54

patently did. For Onslow had now turned back and given Bobby a ferocious scowl. Perhaps it was merely that Bobby (Robert Appleby, scrum-half, Oxford and England) was not yet running to fat. Or perhaps Onslow actually did have memories—and displeasing memories—of Bobby as a small boy. Indeed, Bobby had to confess to himself, this was only too likely. But now Dr Gulliver was speaking again. He seemed a little put out by the *farouche* comportment of his partner.

'Appleby,' Dr Gulliver said, 'has just been mentioning one of our former assistants. That agreeable young fellow Chinn.'

'Nauze,' Bobby said.

'Anglo-Indians, of course, for many generations.' Dr Gulliver was unheeding. 'I recall that Lieutenant-Fireworker Humphrey Chinn—mark, Appleby, that the rank is full of history—assisted an ancestor of my own at the capture of Seringapatam. The date may well be memorised, Appleby. 1799.'

'Do *you* remember Nauze?' It was to Onslow that Bobby addressed this question. There was a possibility that, graceless though he was, Onslow might produce a little more sense than the imbecile Gulliver.

'Nauze? You're barking up the wrong tree. Never had a fellow of that name round here, that I can remember.'

'He taught me Latin. Rather well, as a matter of fact.' Bobby went on to these particulars automatically. It was surely beyond belief that Onslow could have forgotten Nauze's very name. Onslow simply didn't want to talk about him. And Onslow was so desperately thick that he had recourse to this absurd prevarication. For the first time since arriving at Overcombe, Bobby felt alerted to something that might really be there. Chinn, yes; Nauze, no. And if both Gulliver and Onslow chose to forget the latter, it was not at all probable that it was because he had been a trifle heavy-handed in the matter of discipline. Of course there might have been some other sort of scandal, in no way connected with, or leading to, Nauze's ending up—if he *had* ended up—dead on a golf-course. Nauze could have turned into an awful drunk, totally unworthy to instruct the young Beadons of Wiltshire or applaud the speeches of Air-Vice-Marshal Synn-Essery—and his name be consigned to oblivion at Overcombe in consequence.

It was the present representative of the Beadons who terminated this abortive conference. He had looked at his watch (anniversary gift of a devoted aunt, Angela Lady Beadon-Beadon) and was now vigorously massaging his stomach.

'Chop, chop,' Master Beadon said. 'Coolie chaps vellee-vellee hungry. All coolie chaps want chop, chop. Want mungaree.'

'Mungaree, mungaree!' All the infants employed on the Onslow *corvée* took up this mysterious cry, pounding their bellies and contorting their features the while. Bobby had once more to remind himself that all small boys are mad. A well-trained prep-school matron must look out for symptoms of sanity in much the spirit in which she looks out for those of chicken-pox or German measles. And Dr Gulliver, who might have been expected to evince displeasure before this bizarre display, merely nodded benignly.

'*Misce stultitiam consiliis brevem,*' Dr Gulliver said learnedly. '*Dulce est desipere in loco.*'

'Yes, sir.' Bobby found himself once more spontaneously putting on his top-of-the-form turn. '*Neque semper arcum*—is that right, sir?—*Tendit Apollo.*'

'Excellent, Appleby.' Dr Gulliver was highly pleased. 'It is luncheon that our young people are thinking of. And you will join us, I trust, at our simple refection.'

From behind Bobby, disconcertingly, came a sudden half-smothered snarl. It seemed an excessive reaction even on the brutish Onslow's part to an invitation he didn't

56

approve of. But that was what the noise had been about, all the same.

Lunch proved to be another thing that hadn't changed at Overcombe. It was undeniably nutritious, and would doubtless have received the commendations of a visiting dietician, supposing so unlikely a personage ever was to penetrate here. It could not, however, conscientiously have been described as palatable. As mungaree it served well enough; the young gentlemen of Overcombe, delicately bred though they had been in the nurseries of the affluent, shovelled it away with much more vigour than they had applied when excavating for the Long Jump. Dr Gulliver ate with every appearance of informed satisfaction, as if he were a gourmet on a particularly lucky day. His staff saw no reason for any such masquerade; they consumed what was set before them in a sullen gloom suggestive of the Bad Poor in a Victorian workhouse. The meal was thus not informative—or was so only in point of what Bobby could learn by gazing around him.

This was not encouraging. The entire staff of a place like Overcombe of course numbered no more than a dozen, and Bobby saw hardly anybody, apart from the joint proprietors, who was not quite young. Presumably nobody who could help himself stuck this sort of servitude indefinitely. There were two young women who clearly ran the domestic side. These were rather attractive, and might have achieved a good deal of Bobby's attention had he not (in that department of the masculine psyche) been so tied up with the vanished girl. There were two almost middle-aged men whom he somehow guessed hadn't been at the school for long; they looked highly intelligent, and must therefore belong to that class of persons who drift into humble employment through some sheer inability to manage their own lives. They would know nothing about Bloody Nauze. Nor would any of the others. Bobby had certainly never set eyes on any of them before, and they were far too junior to have memories stretching back a dozen years. Or all of them—Bobby suddenly saw—except old Hartsilver.

Old Hartsilver had been the art master—and so not thought of as a master at all. Except when ragging around in the art room, one hadn't much noticed Hartsilver. (Indeed, one hadn't very much noticed him then, either.) And it had taken Bobby all this time to notice him now. He sat at the head of a table given over to the very smallest boys. It looked as if he enjoyed at least one advantage over his colleagues, since he was clearly without any awareness whatever of what he ate. Bobby remembered him as living in a dream. Perhaps it was a dream of the pictures he was never going to paint. For when he was quite a young man something dreadful had begun to happen to Hartsilver's central nervous system—at least Bobby thought it was that—so that his hands had ceased at all adequately to obey his will. Not without evidence of agonising effort, he could control a gross tremor through the seconds necessary for showing a child how to correct the perspective of a cube, or hatch in a shadow, or recover a high-light with an india-rubber. That had been old Hartsilver then, and that was doubtless old Hartsilver now. Because he had been remote and withdrawn and gentle, the boys had teased him mercilessly. At the same time, Bobby now remembered, they had comported themselves with a flawless delicacy in any situation directly involving his disability. Bobby (or rather Robert, promising novelist) felt a sudden envy of those writers—Joyce Cary, Forrest Reid, Richard Hughes, William Golding—who could really 'do' children. There hardly existed a richer, more marvellous world.

But Hartsilver had scarcely slipped within Bobby's observation before he slipped out again. His place was empty; his crumpled table-napkin was being folded by the small boy next to whom he had sat; he himself had departed before the meal had reached its noisy end. Probably by this time Hartsilver didn't even handle knives and forks too well, so that eating in public was a trial to him. But it was something that an art master—the humblest of all ushers in a private school—had to make the best of, no doubt. It seemed to Bobby that it would be civilised to try and have a word with Hartsilver. And of course it looked as if Hartsilver was the one man who might tell him something about Nauze.

Dr Gulliver, it turned out, was minded to say good-bye to his visiting Old Boy at the end of the meal. This was fair enough, even taking into account the fact that he had extracted from Bobby a cheque for five pounds towards the cost of some building-operation which was probably entirely mythical. Headmasters are supposed to be very busy men, and it was proper that Gulliver should sustain that impression of himself. All the same, Bobby had a feeling that he was being invited to clear out less on Gulliver's instance than on Onslow's—and rather as if Onslow had decided that he was less a mere nuisance than some sort of threat. But there seemed no sense in this. Get yourself involved with bodies in bunkers, Bobby told himself, and in no time you are imagining things.

So Bobby made proper remarks to his hosts, got into his car, and drove off. But after a couple of bends on Overcombe's long and ill-kept drive, when he felt that the sound of his engine must have faded away, he drew into the side and came to a halt again. He remembered that what had gone by the grand name of the Art Block in his day had in fact been an old Nissen hut pitched some way from the main building. It seemed improbable that Hartsilver was better or otherwise accommodated now. And nothing would be happening in it at this early hour in the afternoon—one at which the whole school prescriptively took to a disorganised life on its playing-fields. But Hart-

59

silver himself would have gone back to his hut, since the place was the only tolerable refuge he had.

This turned out to be the case. Bobby knocked at the door of the hut, and went in. Hartsilver was alone. He was contemplating a reproduction, pinned up on a wall, of a self-portrait in silver-point drawn by Dürer when he was about thirteen. Dürer was thus much of an age with Hartsilver's present charges at Overcombe. Perhaps Hartsilver was comparing the young Dürer with, say, the young Beadon—something like that. But now Hartsilver, having responded to the knock on his door, was contemplating Bobby precisely as he had been contemplating his reproduction of that marvellously precocious drawing in the Albertina. And at once Bobby remembered that this had been Hartsilver's habit long ago. He had always contrived to see the little savages of Overcombe *not* as little savages but simply as endlessly fascinating plastic entities which, but for the calamity which had befallen him, he might equally endlessly have given his life to arresting on a canvas or a square of paper.

Bobby had forgotten what it was like to be looked at with this particular eye. It was one, he thought, which his mother, so devoted a sculptor, must deliberately refrain from directing upon him. It had a depersonalising effect, so that he wondered how he was to suggest himself to Hartsilver as being something other than a complex visual phenomenon.

'I'm frightfully sorry,' Bobby said, 'but I'm—'

'Bobby.' Hartsilver was smiling gently. 'Bobby Appleby. You were absolutely no good, you know, so that it's odd that I should remember you. You might have been a Mohammedan, for all the ability you had to draw so much as a dog or a cat. Like most of the others, really. Yet there was something a little odd about its being that way with you.' Hartsilver paused in recollection. 'Isn't one of your parents—?'

'My father's a policeman,' Bobby said—and paused mischievously on this false trail.

'Then it was your mother. But you were no credit to her. Yet there was something there. My dear Bobby—if I may still so address you—can it be that you have become a musician?'

'I've become a writer—of a sort.'

'That would be it!' Hartsilver was delighted. 'And is that why you have returned to Overcombe? But no! Your first—or even perhaps your second, would it be?—novel is behind you. So you haven't come back to this desperate place for copy.'

'Well, no—as a matter of fact I haven't.'

'I'm delighted to hear it. I give you notice that I wish positively not to be put in a novel.'

'You won't be by me.' Bobby felt in danger of being possessed by an irrelevant excitement. It was the excitement of finding that he and old Hartsilver had been the same sort of person all the time. And perhaps (despite the gratifying acclaim bestowed by Sunday newspapers upon Robert Appleby, promising author of *The Lumber Room*) —perhaps he was himself going to be as thoroughly unsuccessful as this old creature, lingering out his broken career in a crazy school. But it wouldn't matter. It was the fact that one was an artist that was the important thing.

From these reflections—somewhat sentimental in character, and undeniably irrelevant to the design with which he had returned to Overcombe—Bobby managed to shake himself free.

'I want to ask you something,' he said firmly.

'Really?' It was with an air of surprise that Hartsilver said this. 'I'm very seldom asked anything—except perhaps to give an extra hour to the most unteachable of the children, in order to iron out some difficulty in the time-table. Not that talent doesn't lurk among the unteachable from time to time. Even through the Free Expression occasionally.'

Bobby remembered the Free Expression, and saw that it was still going on. The blackboards had become whiteboards, and the aerial dog-fights once crudely chalked on them had given way to spacecraft and extra-galactic monsters.

'A boy called Beadon, for example,' Hartsilver was saying. 'He has a flair for caricature, and I fear his use of it at times inclines to impertinence. But I haven't the heart to check him. On the board over there.'

Bobby briefly inspected Beadon's productions, since it would have been uncivil to neglect to do so. There was a passable representation of Onslow in a state of inebriety, and underneath it the words:

THE GRATE SOAK OF PETERBOROUGH

Next to this was Hartsilver himself dressed in a juvenile sailor-suit and dancing a hornpipe; this was labelled:

PORTLAND BILL

Finally there was Dr Gulliver, depicted in an attitude of weighty oratory which Bobby recalled clearly enough; he was described as:

THE SELEBRATED SEVERN BORE BORING

'At least,' Bobby said, 'Beadon seems to be making progress with his Geography. He just has to catch up a little in Spelling, and he'll be a credit to the school. But what I want to ask you is this: do you remember a man called Nauze?'

'Nauze?' For a moment it was almost as if Hartsilver had an impulse to shy away from the name. If this was so, however, he recovered himself. 'Dear me, yes. He was here in your time, was he not? You had a nickname for him: Bleeding Nauze.'

'Bloody Nauze.'

'To be sure. He was a little too fond of telling boys to touch their toes.'

'That's right—but not in the least to any point of scandal. But *was* there a scandal? Connected, I mean, with his leaving Overcombe.'

'I might have been the last to hear of anything of the sort. I am not a great frequenter of our staff common room. I do have an impression, however, that Nauze left rather abruptly.' Hartsilver was looking at Bobby in some surprise, and perhaps not altogether without disapproval. This was fair enough, since there wasn't much propriety in an Old Boy's seeming attempt to get idle gossip going in this way. But at least Hartsilver now went on quite readily. 'It must have been not long after you left Overcombe yourself, so Nauze might well have faded from my mind. As a matter of fact, however, I recall him fairly vividly.'

'Do you remember something about one of his hands?'

'He had a finger missing, of course. And that is perhaps a thing that a boy would be particularly likely to keep in mind. But he was notable for something quite other than any mere physical characteristic. Nauze was a remarkable man. I believe I'd call him a *very* remarkable man.' Hartsilver paused. 'His intellectual endowment was in some respects truly outstanding.'

'Then why do you think he—' Bobby broke off in some confusion, since he had been about to employ some such form of words as 'came down to working in this cock-eyed school'. His discomfort was, if anything, increased by noticing that Hartsilver was smiling gently.

'Perhaps, Bobby, the poor man had a past. How lucky one is oneself not to have had that. It makes not having a

future a good deal more bearable. I don't mean that Nauze
—and I wonder why you are interested in him?—was the
kind of man who might have left behind him anything
really memorable. There are kinds of genius of whom one
never feels that. And no end of people of the first ability.
Think of them, Bobby: all the professors and judges, the
Kunsthistoriker, the Ministers of the Crown, the top civil
servants.'

'Yes, of course.' Bobby found this sudden gentle arrogance disconcerting. 'But was this chap Nauze, gym-shoe
and all, getting on for being a genius?'

'Shall I just say that he had a brilliant mind—more brilliant even than Dr Gulliver himself?' Hartsilver had turned
from arrogance to whimsical malice. Suddenly—and most
surprisingly—he shot out a question. 'Why have you
hunted me out, Bobby, to ask questions about Nauze?'

'I believe he may be dead. I believe he may have died in
rather a horrible way. And that other people—or another
person—may be in danger as a result of having been ...
well, in at the kill. So I want to find out about him.'

During this quite short speech, Hartsilver had contrived
to drift away. Bobby remembered this as a physical necessity of his. In the middle of quite relaxed talk, the old man
would be unaccountably impelled to get out of at least
touching distance of anybody else. At the moment he had
returned to Dürer's drawing of the prep-school Dürer, and
was seemingly as absorbed in it as if he had never seen it
before. But when he turned round it was to continue the
conversation naturally enough.

'My dear Bobby, this is most distressing. Did you say
your father was a policeman?'

'Yes.'

'I'm being silly, my dear boy. Even I used to notice Sir
John Appleby's name in the news often enough. Are you
turning detective because the role of Crown Prince is
attractive to you?'

64

'I don't think so.' The sharpness of this had taken Bobby by surprise. 'As a matter of fact, the person who may be in danger is a girl. It's a little difficult to explain.'

'Then let us simply return to Nauze. It would be extravagant to call him a genius. But at least he had an astounding linguistic faculty. I'd be surprised to hear that, when he had a pupil with the elements of docility, he didn't teach Latin rather well.'

'He certainly did that. I never saw him after I was about thirteen. But it was Nauze who got me my First in Mods seven years later. Incidentally, he started me on my Greek as well, and equally effectively. And I can remember having a dim sense that he'd never himself *done* Greek.'

'Precisely. Do you do the crossword puzzle in *The Times*?'

'Only when my father makes me help him. My father's a fifteen to twenty minute man on it.'

'Nauze's average time was seven and a half minutes.'

'That's not possible.'

'It was to Nauze. And he was equally good at various sorts of mathematical puzzle.'

'I see. Did he show off?'

'Far from it. His expertness was more like something that he betrayed in spite of himself. The betrayal had something to do with his drinking a great deal.'

'The boys never knew anything about that.' Bobby frowned. 'Except—do you know?—when he had those bouts with the gym shoe—and they were essentially bouts —we felt there was something funny about him.'

'He had been drinking. It released certain inhibitions, no doubt. I believe that's the word.'

'It's rather revolting.' Bobby discovered that he did feel genuinely revolted. 'Of course, it's an utterly trivial thing. A chap extracting a harmless sort of yelp from small boys just because he's had a pint too much. Disagreeable, all the same. Yet I rather liked Nauze. I believe that most of us did. I suppose he gave us a good conceit of ourselves. We overestimated the merit gained by passing through that mild ordeal.' Bobby fell silent for a moment. 'But all this is nonsense—unless it gives me a better picture of the man. I want to *see* Nauze clearly. In my head, I mean.'

'You mean you don't recollect his appearance?'

'I thought I did. It would never have occurred to me that I couldn't visualise him clearly enough, supposing that it had come into my head to do so. But now, when I have had occasion to try, I see something shadowy and elusive— hovering behind the pointing finger that wasn't there.'

'Most interesting. Would you go so far as to say, Bobby, that if he walked into the room now you mightn't be quite sure of him?'

'Oh, I don't think so. That would be quite incredible. Unless, of course he had changed a great deal. And people do change enormously in twelve years.'

'It rather depends on *what* twelve years.' Hartsilver had been gazing at the door of his Nissen hut rather as if he expected Bloody Nauze actually to appear. 'Bobby Appleby has changed quite a lot. But have I?' Hartsilver's gentle smile flitted over his face and vanished. 'You already saw me as on the last verge of my confine.'

'You haven't changed much.' Bobby spoke rather shortly—partly because he had almost said 'You're astonishingly well-preserved', and partly because he was becoming impatient for some real discovery.

'Of course there are the photographs. You remember them? A group photograph, taken every year. Through Dr Gulliver's great kindness, we all get a copy. I confess to having no impulse to range them on my wall. But it would be indecent to destroy them. So they're in a portfolio —there by the far window.'

Hartsilver had untied the tapes of the portfolio and hoisted it on an easel. It was the way he had sometimes

shown you colour-prints and photographs if you had wandered round to the Art Block alone or with one or two
other boys. It had been almost a covert activity—or at
least you didn't too readily let it get around that a holy
awe befell you when you gazed upon the productions of
people with names like Michelangelo and Piero della
Francesca. Bobby understood that matters were different
at many prep schools now, and that a precocious cultiva-
tion of aesthetic experience was all the go at them. He
doubted whether this was so at Overcombe. Dr Gulliver
and Mr Onslow, in point of both the theory and practise
of education, were conservatively disposed.

There was no occasion for holy awe before the group
photographs, although they weren't in fact to be contemplated entirely without some sort of emotion. Bobby
had his own collection of such things at Dream, although
they now reposed in an abandoned suitcase in an attic.
Some were even of a pre-Overcombe-era: kindergarten
memorials, or Bobby doing ballet with horrible little girls
at Miss Kimp's Academy of the Dance. After Overcombe
there came the whole saga of his progress through his
public school, ending up with Elevens, Fifteens, Prefects,
and—ultimate pinnacle—*solus* between the headmaster
and the headmaster's wife in commemoration of his having become Head Boy. Then, at Oxford, the whole thing
starting again, but with new sorts of relics creeping in:
the menus of dining clubs, for example, or of banquets
given by the affluent to celebrate their majority. It all
reeked of privilege, Bobby would tell himself, and all
these fond κειμήλια should be consigned to a bonfire. But
they hadn't been—only to an attic. Bobby, who was an
extremely honest young man, had to tell himself that, if
God were to let him choose, he wouldn't want to have had
a day of it different. Very obscurely, it had accumulated
some sort of debt, and not one which you at all discharged
by becoming an agreeably esteemed tiro novelist.

These were serious thoughts, wholly inapposite to the sort of thriller or adventure story which Bobby was so anxious to see begin stirring round him. He did his best to scrutinise the Overcombe school photographs as his father might once have scrutinised such things at Scotland Yard. Year after year, they had all been taken in the same spot—before the slightly bogus Georgian portico which was the most impressive feature of the large ramshackle house. The same forms had been dragged out into the open air and disposed in the same shallow arc. But the only other constants were Hartsilver himself, Dr Gulliver, and Mr Onslow. The last, indeed, was constant only in minor degree. For whereas Hartsilver's best suit was mysteriously as shabby in any one year as in any other, and Dr Gulliver was undeviatingly attired in his cap and gown, Mr Onslow never appeared as quite the same character twice. He could be estimated, for example, as putting on about half a stone yearly, while his clothes and accoutrements suggested a kind of scholastic Proteus. Rugger balls, Soccer balls, cricket bats, hockey sticks, tennis rackets, boxing gloves, fencing foils, vaulting poles, and the like passed with him in a kind of heraldic procession down the years.

The rest of the staff—academic or domestic, male or female—hinted a fairly brisk turnover. So, of course, did the boys. Any individual was first to be found in a row crouching cross-legged at the staff's feet, then on tiptoe on a hazardously improvised scaffolding at the back, after that on a similar contraption on a lower level, and finally seated in a secure dignity on one or another flank of the grown-ups. Apart from this, the boys seemed to fall into two main groups. There were those who stuck out their chests and glowered defiantly at the camera; and there were those who contrived a species of concave or inward-turning stance and were chiefly evocative of small creatures of burrowing habit deprived for the time of their natural refuge. Bobby saw that he had himself been a child of the chest-protruding order.

'There he is.'

Hartsilver, instead of waiting for Bobby to identify Nauze for himself, had placed a finger on one of the photographs.

'I'd have known him at once.' Bobby was able to speak with conviction, for it had instantly become incredible that Bloody Nauze's features could ever have become dim to him. 'He doesn't look much at home, does he? But this is the first one in which he appears. And it's only two years before I do.'

'And three years later he has departed.' Hartsilver was thumbing forward through the photographs. 'How often, I wonder, has he come into my head since then? Not often. Now you say he may be dead, and I reply that the news distresses me. A mere convention of speech, I fear. But does it strike you that some of these boys may be dead too? Indeed, it's a certainty. Disease has faltered in its attack upon the young, no doubt. But the motor-car and the motor-cycle have taken over.'

'I suppose so.' Bobby didn't think much of this gratuitous mortuary reflection. 'But I'm more concerned about the girl. I told you there was a girl. *She* may be dead. If she is, I shan't readily forgive myself.' Bobby paused, and noticed that Hartsilver had come to the end of fingering over the photographs. 'Is that last year's?'

'Yes. These are the people you met at lunch.'

'Not all of them. There's a bald-headed man with a squint in this photograph. I didn't see him.'

'Ah, poor Rushout. He suffered from chronomania, and left hurriedly.'

'Chronomania?'

'A charitable term invented by myself, Bobby. Rushout took to going round the dormitories in the small hours and possessing himself of the boys' watches. And he didn't return them. Dr Gulliver, who is of course a man of the very highest moral probity, decided that it really wouldn't quite do.'

'I see. And there are three young women in the photograph, but there were only two at lunch. I suppose—' Bobby broke off abruptly, and suddenly pointed with a trembling finger. *That one—who is she?*'

'Ah, that one. Her name—' Hartsilver too broke off, but only because there had been a knock at the door of his hut. 'Come in.'

Then it happened. The door opened, and a young woman was revealed in a strong shaft of sunlight. She was the third young woman in the photograph. And she was the girl as well.

CHAPTER FOUR

'You!' Bobby exclaimed.

It was the only conceivable thing to say—or ejaculation to utter. The girl's appearance, after all, was very much a *coup de théâtre*. For one thing, the sunlight was behaving precisely as it had done before, and what Bobby saw— what, alarmingly, he recognised—was the girl as if she had stood virtually naked before him. Once more, it was a figure before a voice. The effect lasted, indeed, only for a moment—for the girl, as if aware of it, stepped rapidly into the hut and closed the door. In this moment she said nothing. She glanced at Bobby fleetingly and with gravity. Then she turned to Hartsilver, with a hint of politely dissimulated surprise on her face.

'Are you busy?' she asked.

'By no means, my dear.' Hartsilver seemed delighted at the girl's arrival. 'I am merely receiving a visit from an old pupil. You would have met him at lunch if you hadn't been away. This is Mr Appleby. Bobby, let me introduce you to Miss Danbury, one of our house-mothers.'

'How do you do?' the girl said. She spoke a shade coolly, as if not entirely disposed to pass over the fact that the young man thus presented to her had behaved bizarrely.

Bobby was dumbfounded—so much so that for a second his surface awareness was confined to the irrelevant reflection that calling young women house-mothers must be one of Overcombe's notably few concessions to the march of time. Then it struck him that the sunlight had put on another disconcerting turn. That was it. The girl had come indoors from a blaze of it, and he himself must be in some sort of half-shadow which had prevented recognition. He took a couple of steps forward—so precipitately that they brought him awkwardly close to the girl's person. So he hastily shoved out a hand, which of course was more awkward still. The girl's expression didn't change. Bobby heard himself say 'How do you do?' in an idiotic manner. There was a moment's silence.

'I suppose I only came in to gossip,' Miss Danbury said to Hartsilver. Her tone was wholly easy and unaffected. 'But there is something I want to ask you. I've found a small boy crying bitterly because he can't draw his dog. He has a dog at home, and he's been trying to draw it— and colour it too—so as to gain a little moral support from it. But he can't make the thing *look* like his dog. Do you think you could help him to produce something that *will* be his dog? He does need comforting, poor little chap. It's his first term.' The girl turned to Bobby. 'Mr Appleby, did you pine for a pet when you were a new boy here?'

This competent manner of receiving Bobby into grace through a little polite conversation didn't please Bobby at all. He even found himself resenting the mere suggestion that he could ever have pined for a pet. So he glowered at the girl in a manner that would have been wholly embarrassing if Hartsilver hadn't been saying that he could certainly draw any individual dog to order, even if he had never seen the brute; and that the distressed infant might present himself for this purpose immediately after prep.

These benevolent remarks at least gave Bobby time to think. Perhaps (he was sometimes to reflect a little later) they even gave him time to imagine things. Hadn't Miss Danbury's cool look also been *a warning look*? Wasn't she —doubtless for some good reason—anxious that her first strange encounter with Bobby should be kept secret at present? Here was the truth—or a fragment of it—at last. they could be sure of privacy. Having realised this, Bobby Not a flicker of recognition was to pass between them until tried to catch Miss Danbury's eye. Having caught it, he gave Miss Danbury a meaning look. Receiving no response to this, he gave her—certainly rashly—a swift wink. Miss Danbury failed to wink in reply. Instead, she turned away from Bobby through an agle of some thirty degrees. Bobby realised—with the effect of a poet rediscovering life in a dead metaphor—that this was what is called being given the cold shoulder. Miss Danbury conversed with Mr Hartsilver on current Overcombe affairs. As Miss Danbury was certainly not an ill-bred girl, the implication of this was clear. Bobby shook hands with Hartsilver, gave Miss Danbury a kind of Jane Austen bow, and retreated from the Art Block with dignity.

He wasn't, of course, going to be defeated. Indeed, there was no question of anything of the sort. It was merely (he told himself, his confidence returning) that this girl was giving him points in the discreet handling of the difficult and almost certainly dangerous situation in which they both found themselves. What he had to do now (if he wasn't further to make a fool of himself) was *to read her mind*. What did she expect him to do? The answer wasn't hard to arrive at. *Lurk*. He must lurk until she could get colourably clear of poor old Hartsilver. Then they could confer, and each discover where the other stood.

For a moment Bobby paused irresolutely just outside the miserable hut which represented Overcombe's concession to the aesthetic side of (juvenile) human nature. He had better not move out of sight of its door. He must conceal himself in a spot from which, upon the girl's emergence, he could attract her attention unobtrusively. Perhaps with a low whistle.

Bobby looked about him. The Art Block stood on somewhat lower ground than the main school buildings, and at some remove from them. Quite close to it, and a little lower still, were the surface evidences of the out-size septic tank which represented Overcombe's advance towards the concepts of modern sanitation. (The school lay a couple of miles from a by-road, let alone from any main drainage.) The delicacy of Dr Gulliver—as of Mr Onslow, no doubt— had caused this humble *necessarium* to be surrounded with a sizable if somewhat suburban-looking privet hedge. The privet hedge, Bobby reflected inconsequently, afforded a good deal more privacy than was enjoyed by the privies which here achieved their easement into external Nature. The horrible things—he suddenly vividly remembered— didn't even have doors. In upper-class English schools, indecency is regarded as the sole effective preventive of immorality ... Upon this sombre thought, Bobby dived behind the hedge.

He didn't have to wait long—perhaps not long enough to do such thinking as he might have done. The door of the hut opened, and the girl appeared. The sun, of course, was now in her face, and for a moment Bobby (who was peering very cautiously through his hedge) saw her pucker her eyes. It wasn't an action that should have conduced to any overwhelming impression of beauty. But it struck Bobby that way. Miss Danbury was a deliriously good-looking girl. And, of course, she had that figure too. Bobby knew he wasn't easily going to forget it.

He wondered whether she was looking around for him. It would be the rational thing to do. But in fact Miss Danbury was now stepping out quite briskly, which was disconcerting. Then he saw that she had taken a path which came straight towards his hiding-place. She must have guessed instantly where he had taken cover. A clever girl. He and she—Bobby told himself—might make quite a formidable team.

But Miss Danbury didn't pause as she drew abreast of him. She walked on regardless, and in a moment would have left the septic tank behind her. So there was nothing for it but to bob up. Bobby bobbed up.

'Hullo!' he said. 'It's me. Come in here.'

At least this halted Miss Danbury in her tracks. Bobby had a notion that she looked alarmed. Perhaps she was judging him to be acting rashly once more.

'It's all right,' he said reassuringly. 'Nobody will see us.'

'Mr Appleby, you must be quite mad.' The girl at least wasn't so alarmed as to take to her heels. 'For all I know, you may be accustomed to conduct your low amours in a ditch. But a cesspool really surprises me. Good afternoon.'

'Stop!' Bobby must have put into this cry passion of a sort other than that which the young woman had apprehended in him. For she did stop—at a safe distance, indeed —and look at him. She looked at him rather carefully.

'Well?' Miss Danbury said.

It didn't seem to Bobby that *she* could be mad, despite her extraordinary conduct. But perhaps she had lost her memory. Indeed, it was very probable that something of that kind had occurred. The affair at the bunker must have been a terrific shock for a sheltered girl like this—apprehensive of improper suggestions when one spoke to her rationally across a hedge. The whole horrible episode must have suppressed itself in her mind. So naturally she was bewildered. The essential thing was to find some gentle means of assisting her to recover from this amnesia.

'I'm frightfully sorry,' Bobby said. 'I'm afraid you must find me very strange. But have you no memory of our having met before?'

'None whatever. And, if I had, it could hardly be of a kind to licence you in this ... this outbreak of lavatory humour.'

'I suppose it is rather an unsuitable place for a conversation with a comparative stranger. Shall we go somewhere else?'

'Rubbish!' With marked feminine inconsequence, Miss Danbury suddenly pushed through the hedge, and confronted Bobby on the broad concrete expanse of the septic tank. It was an elaborate affair of its kind. Here and there a species of fat concrete pipe broke surface, doubled on itself at a height of about two feet, and disappeared again into the Tartarean world below. The effect was of a school of petrified dolphins disporting themselves on a petrified sea. On one of these Miss Danbury sat down. 'Just where,' she asked, 'did we meet before?'

'It was in a bunker.'

'In a bunker!'

'Well, beside a bunker. What *was* in the bunker—I don't want this to be too much of a shock to you—was a dead body.'

'Dear me! Just whose dead body, Mr Appleby?' The girl was now looking at Bobby very steadily indeed—rather as one is told to look at a lion or tiger if it shows signs of giving trouble.

'That's just what I don't know. Or not for certain. You see, the body disappeared again.'

'Of course.' Miss Danbury appeared to give this whole difficult business some moments' thought. 'Mr Appleby, is your home far from here?'

'It's at a place called Long Dream, near Linger. Perhaps you remember Linger?' Bobby produced this almost coaxingly. 'About a hundred miles away.'

'I see.' Miss Danbury paused, and then added casually, 'Can you give me your telephone number?'

'What on earth—'

'I'd like you to allow me to ring up whoever is at Dream —your wife, or parents, or whoever it may be. Because, you see, I don't think you're very well. Please don't think me impertinent. And I don't expect it's very serious. But I do feel you should be in competent hands. Have you a reliable family doctor at Dream?'

This professional house-motherly solicitude did at least a little clear Bobby's head. If the girl was wrong in supposing him astray in his wits it was only reasonable to

76

admit that he might be equally wrong in supposing some aberration of the memory or the like to have befallen hers. So what other hypothesis could make sense of this extraordinary situation?

'Listen,' Bobby said urgently. 'Tell me this. Have you got a double?'

'A double? How on earth should I know? There must be plenty of people totally unknown to us, I imagine, to whom we bear a more or less close resemblance. Your question simply isn't a sensible one, Mr Appleby.'

'That's perfectly true. So let me ask another. Have you a twin sister?'

'Certainly not!' The girl shot out this reply with an asperity which seemed to surprise her.

'I know I must seem to be behaving very impertinently, Miss Danbury. By the way, my name is Bobby.' Bobby paused hopefully on this, but it was rather markedly that nothing came of it. 'But surely you can see that I'm not really mad. Isn't that so?'

'I don't know *what* is so.' For the first time, the girl seemed not quite to know her own mind. 'Perhaps you are simply under some misapprehension that can be cleared up. When you think you saw me before, was it for *long* that you saw me?'

'Far from it. I simply—'

'And it was when something upsetting had happened— or at least something distracting? Don't you think that, as a consequence, you have probably made a mistake? We know that very odd things can happen over questions of identity, when there has been a question of a crime or something of the sort. People go to police stations and pick out—'

'I want to know your name.'

'I don't see the slightest occasion—'

'I want to know your name, please.'

'It's Susan.'

'Susan, listen. Why can't you trust me? Why can't you trust me, instead of talking nonsense and involving yourself in awkward lies? I'm sorry, but I've suddenly got this quite clear. The mere fact of the matter, I mean. On Tuesday morning, you and I were standing beside each other on the golf-course at Linger. And there was a dead man—a murdered man, almost certainly—within three yards of us. You know that's true. Admit it, and we may get somewhere. Go on denying it, and you may put yourself in a very difficult position.'

'You talk like a policeman, Mr Appleby. I've no doubt you were on a golf-course. And I've no doubt some woman was too. If you say there was a dead man, I accept it. Dead men exist, and perhaps they even turn up in bunkers from time to time. Only the woman wasn't me.'

'Listen again, please. I haven't come to Overcombe by chance. There was something about the dead man—and you know what it was, I think—that suggested somebody who had been here when I was a boy. So I came over to see if I could pick up some sort of trail. And what I have found is you—Susan Danbury, who vanished, just as the body did, from the golf-course at Linger. What have you to say to that?'

'I'm not required to say anything ... Bobby Appleby.' The girl had sprung to her feet with flashing eyes—but at the same time with so extreme a pallor flooding—if pallor can flood—her face that Bobby wondered whether she was going to faint.

And then a very dreadful thing happened. Bobby suddenly found himself wondering whether he was going to faint instead. Equally suddenly, a flash of self-knowledge told him why. Ever since the thing on the golf-course happened, he had been fooling around with this girl inside his head. And, until this very moment, it had all been nonsense: a rather messy fudging up of romantic feeling about a young woman encountered in gruesome circumstances.

78

The same young woman was now before him—indicted of lies, striken by some ghastly and guilty predicament. And Bobby loved her deeply. She had been Rosaline on the golf course. She was Juliet now.

CHAPTER FIVE

SHE HAD WALKED away, and Bobby was left to consult his own troubled mind. He had to ask himself why he wasn't running after her, shouting that they mustn't part like this. It was essentially because of a sudden conviction that, if he wasn't to proceed with her on what might prove some fatally wrong assumption, he must give himself time to think. But of course the person professionally equipped to do the sort of thinking that seemed required—thinking about a darkening mystery in a context of what appeared to be revolting crime—was his father. So his first impulse to action was simply to get into his car again and drive hard for Dream.

Perhaps Bobby had decided against this in the very moment that he had sat down—for he *had* sat down—on the curly pipe on which Susan Danbury had been sitting moments before. To go home would be to decamp, and this was something he mustn't do. For Overcombe had become, incredible as it seemed, a sinister place. He was in no doubt of this at all, although it wasn't anything which could be called thinking that had brought him to such a conclusion. Something instinctive and irrational was at play upon him. Or if there were objective reasons for his feeling, they belonged to that category of clues and signals which slip into the mind without being consciously registered—and which produce (he had heard his father say) what is popularly called a hunch. He had a hunch about Overcombe. It seemed a very strange place to have a hunch about.

He mustn't drive away—unless he could take Susan Danbury along with him. And Susan had shown no disposition whatever to treat him as a knight errant. There was no reason why she should. 'What have you to say to that?' he had demanded, hastily and aggressively, for all the world like some Detective Branch policeman whom his father would never have tipped as likely to go far. At this thought Bobby jumped to his feet—the outcropping sewage machinery wasn't at all comfortable, anyway—and paced up and down the ridiculous concrete expanse he had so ham-handedly chosen for the recent *rencontre*. When he and Susan were married, they would have to recollect that their first meeting had been in company with a corpse, and their second on top of a monstrous cloaca. *For love has played his mansion in the place of excrement.* ... As this observation by his favourite poet came into Bobby's head, Bobby had to admit to himself that perhaps he was going crazy. For one thing, he wasn't remotely likely to marry Susan Danbury. She just wasn't going to feel about him in that sort of way. As for how he felt about her—well, that was a matter of a hard core of conviction at present surrounded by layers of the most appalling bewilderment.

He knew nothing whatever about her—except that here she was, and that she was employed at Overcombe to ensure that Master Beadon and his contemporaries washed behind their ears. And no doubt the bunch of tenth-rate ushers employed to staff the place on its scholastic side were constantly making passes at her. Bobby remembered with horror that evidences of the same sort of thing long ago had been a topic for ribaldry among the more knowing of the young gentlemen under Dr Gulliver's tutelage. But this was an irrelevant thought, and he swopped it for the reflection that if he had made a poor job of learning almost anything about Susan he had scarcely done much better in the case of Nauze. He now knew when Nauze had left the school, and he had been told something about the man's abilities and habits which he hadn't known before. Nauze had possessed what Hartsilver described as an astounding linguistic faculty; he had been skilled at cross-word puzzles and mathematical problems; he had drunk a great deal; he had perhaps left Overcombe rather abruptly. This was a meagre gathering. Was there anything else that he had learnt about Nauze?

Nauze had been the man in the bunker. When Bobby had arrived at Overcombe, he had brought with him a mere hypothesis. He would take away a certainty.

Abandoning the septic tank and making his way slowly back to his car, Bobby checked over this proposition. It turned, of course, upon the two appearances of the girl: first by the bunker, and now here. For if the body in the bunker had *not* been that of Nauze then Bobby's trip to Overcombe had been, so to speak, entirely at random. And that such a random trip should have brought him up against the girl again was quite astronomically unlikely; one had only to think of the total population and the geographical limits of the British Isles to see that the chances against such a further encounter were a good many million to one.

But what did this tell him about the girl? What did it tell him about her relationship with Nauze? Almost nothing—Bobby quickly saw—that was quite assured and certain.

Susan Danbury was now employed at a school where Nauze had once been employed. But Nauze had ceased so to be employed years and years ago—and Susan was clearly so young that she herself couldn't have been at Overcombe for very long. So here was a very tenuous link indeed. And there was only one other real link. Three days before, and a hundred miles from Overcombe, Susan had turned up from nowhere when Bobby was in the act of discovering a dead man on a golf-course. Then Susan had vanished—to turn up at Overcombe, a place Bobby had found reason to associate with the corpse. The body had vanished as well. *Might it perhaps turn up at Overcombe too?*

They had been felling some of the over-mature beeches in the long winding avenue to the school. Bobby found that he had sat down abruptly on a stump. It was at least more comfortable than one of those curly pipes. But he might probably have sat down on a thorn-tree without much being aware of the fact. The fantastic question he had just so inconsequently asked himself had pretty well laid him out.

He had better ask himself something more sensible. Wasn't there at least one possibility which, although it postulated stiff coincidence, didn't postulate coincidence of the virtually inconceivable order he had just felt obliged to reject? *Susan, who worked at Overcombe, had been present, entirely by chance, on the occasion of the discovering of the body of a man who had worked at Overcombe long ago.* Bobby paused on this, and saw that he had to add something else. *And again, entirely by chance, the discoverer of the body—one Robert Appleby—had been at Overcombe as well.* Gloomily, Bobby had to conclude that he was again in the region of astronomical improbability, after all.

And these mental gymnastics—which weren't even as clear-headed as they ought to be—he had been undertaking in the interest of letting Susan out. That was the only way to express the thing. He wanted the girl to be entirely innocent of something—and without himself precisely knowing what that something was.

In a kind of desperation now, Bobby tried one final notion. It was at least a very simple one. *There were two girls.*

This, after all, was what Susan herself had suggested. Bobby was mistaken in supposing that the girl who had come into Hartsilver's hut was the girl who had briefly stood beside him at the bunker. He had been involved in something nasty, and had got round to imagining things. It hadn't perhaps been very tactful of Susan to suggest he should see a doctor. But ought he at least, so to speak, to see an oculist?

No good. No good at all. One coincidence, indeed, you could get rid of in terms of it. The body discovered by Robert Appleby, Overcombe Old Boy, need *not* have been that of Bloody Nauze, Overcombe ex-master. But consider. Appleby, Overcombe Old Boy, discovers body minus one finger as Nauze, Overcombe ex-master, was minus one finger: this in the presence of Girl *A*. Appleby proceeds to Overcombe and encounters Girl *B*—who he is instantly convinced *is* Girl *A*. There is a certain plausibility about this explanation, and Girl *B* has urged it. When you go to parties, for example, you sometimes meet somebody whom you are quite convinced you have already met shortly before—and yet this proves to have been impossible. But this, of course, was a very imperfect analogy indeed. Bobby had made his way from the bunker to Overcombe (you might put in) with Girl *A* very, very much on his mind. And at Overcombe he had first instantly, and then obstinately and with unfaltering conviction, accepted Girl *B* as *being* Girl *A*. It was quite inconceivable that, by mere chance, there should be—here at Overcombe—a second girl so like the first girl that any simple misidentification on his part was possible. If the two girls were *not* the same girl then Bobby was very mad indeed, and Susan had been more than justified in those inquiries about his family doctor.

At this point, and while still sitting gloomily on the stump of the beech, Bobby felt in his pocket for his pipe and tobacco-pouch. Then suddenly he was aware that this impulse had come to him through some kind of sympathetic response to the fact that there was tobacco-smoke in the air already. A dim memory stirred in him. He got up, crossed the avenue, and dropped into a concealed hollow on the other side. Before him, comfortably sprawled on springy turf, were two of Dr Gulliver's charges. It was clear that they had withdrawn from the afternoon's athletic occasions for the purposes of an unholy joy. It was a delicious aroma of Turkish tobacco that was in the air. Master Beadon was one of the two sybaritic infants producing it.

'Hullo!' Bobby said. 'Do you mind if I smoke a very plain sort of pipe?'

'We shall be delighted, of course.' Beadon, although a displeasing vision of chatisement at the hand of an outraged Doctor must have been hovering before him, answered with a *sang-froid* of which Angela Lady Beadon-Beadon would undoubtedly have approved in her favourite nephew.

Bobby sat down, lit the pipe, and surveyed the two boys as candidly as they were surveying him. In terms of what he recalled of school-stories, they ought both to show complexions beginning to turn a nasty green. Nothing of the kind, however, was observable, and what he had come upon was one of those states of blissful and contented ease which talented twelve-year-olds do acquire skill in carving out of their scurrying, clamorous and harried lives. *Alas! unconscious of their fate, the little victims play.* Momentarily, a sharp nostalgia again smote Bobby Appleby.

'This,' Beadon said on a detectable note of social reproach, 'is Walcot Major.'

'How do you do?' The second small boy made this inquiry with reserve—rather, perhaps, as his mother might make it of a new neighbour of doubtful provenance encountered after Matins outside her parish church.

'How do you do?' Bobby said gravely to Walcot Major. 'My name is Bobby Appleby. I was at Overcombe.'

'We know.' Beadon appeared now to be aiming at a more relaxed atmosphere. 'Some muddied oaf recognised you at lunch. He says you played scrum-half for England a long time ago. Is that so?'

'Well, yes.' Bobby was rather startled by this vision of

85

the years rolling over him.

'I *suppose* that explains your coming back.' Beadon looked doubtful, even suspicious. 'I've noticed it's done mostly by people who make games their principal thing. Walcot has an older brother like that. An earlier Walcot Major.'

'He's putting on weight,' Walcot said with obscure satisfaction. 'Like our poor old thickie, F.L. It's what happens to muscle, if you go in for it.'

'So I've been told,' Bobby said humbly.

'But you look to be keeping your form fairly well.' Beadon said agreeably. 'Do you still go for runs and things?'

'Sometimes.' Bobby perceived that he was in the presence of the intransigent intellectuals of Overcombe. He recalled with wonder Master Beadon putting on that coolie-turn for Onslow's benefit. It seemed almost a *trahison des clercs.* 'And,' Bobby added, 'I play golf.'

'You'll be able to go on doing that for a number of years, I should think.' Walcot's tone seemed to aim at judicious felicitation. 'If all goes well,' he added. 'Do you drink much?'

'No. And I don't smoke cigarettes. Just this pipe two or three times a day.'

This produced a brief silence. Beadon had rolled over on his stomach, his chin cupped comfortably in his hands, and his heels kicking in air. He was almost unnervingly like an illustration from some outmoded juvenile fiction— *The Fifth Form at St Dominic's*, or perhaps *Teddy Lester's Schooldays.* He appeared to have taken up this position for the purpose of subjecting Bobby to closer appraisal.

'You don't seem to me to be quite the type,' Beadon said firmly.

'The type?' Bobby was startled.

'I'm interested in types. You see, I draw them.'

'Yes, I know. Portland Bill, and the Severn Bore. I was

admiring them.'

'Oh, that's all rot.' The self-possessed Beadon was suddenly overwhelmed with confusion by this compliment. 'A man can't really do anything with bits of chalk. I want to go and be in a studio in Paris, as a matter of fact. With somebody like Daumier. Do you know Daumier? I don't mean I don't realise he's dead. With just that sort of artist. But my parents say I'm still rather too young.'

'I suppose it's a matter of the age in which we live,' Bobby offered gravely. 'At the Renaissance, people like Michelangelo were already going great guns at round about your age. Nowadays it's not thought healthy to be precocious like that.'

'There you are!' Beadon was triumphant. 'You may be a Rugger tough, but you do understand about these things. I knew you were one of us.'

It was when he received this handsome promotion into the intellectual classes that it occurred to Bobby that he might learn something useful from these children. Beadon was bright. Walcot had perhaps the role of Beadon's follower, but this didn't mean that he mightn't be brighter still. They must both be among the oldest generation of boys now at Overcombe, which meant that they had been observing the place for a period of anything up to four years. Much, of course, escapes the observation or understanding of even very acute small boys. A surprising amount does not.

The acuteness of Beadon was already evidenced in the fact that he had detected something odd in Bobby's having turned up at Overcombe at all. This perfectly appeared in the boy's considering gaze now. If Bobby started questioning him rashly, he would quickly sense that he was being pumped, and might resent the fact, or turn wary. At an English preparatory school, after all, the sons of the polite classes lead a life in which survival depends upon behaviour closely approximating to that obtaining among primitive tribes in a jungle. Even at moments in which an agreeable indolence has been achieved, a sudden occasion for cunning may lurk round the next tree. But if Messrs Beadon and Walcot were liable to turn reticent under questioning, they might become quite expansive if craftily lured into showing off. And Bobby didn't feel any scruples about turning crafty. He wasn't in a situation in which one could afford to be over-nice in such matters.

But he must know what he wanted. Without that, all the skill of a Machiavelli would get him nowhere at all. And it was when he realised what he *did* want that a sense of scruple threatened to overcome him. He didn't want— or, rather, he didn't hope for—information about Bloody Nauze. Nauze's name wouldn't linger even as a legend at Overcombe among boys of the Beadon-Walcot generation. He wanted information about Susan Danbury. He wanted to get tabs on her. This was very shocking. Indeed, it was almost unimaginable. He had to take a deep breath even to think of it. But the cold fact was that his divinity (as she might conventionally be called) had walked out on him after pretty well refusing to utter. Something in her position made it impossible for her to confide in him. If he was going to help her—which had become his mission in life—he was thrown on his own resources. He was thrown, indeed, on his own wits. There wasn't even a convenient sea-monster, in fee to Poseidon, whom he could simply take a swipe at and so free his Andromeda from the rock. If there was a vulnerable dragon around, St George as yet lacked a glimpse of so much as its flailing tail. Eventually the role of Perseus or St George might descend upon him. At present he was just a detective, as his father had been.

'I suppose,' Bobby said, 'that Overcombe has changed a great deal since my time.'

'Oh, really? I can't see why it should.' Rather unexpectedly, it was Walcot who took the initiative in offering this reply. 'It's a conservative place, to which conservative parents send us. It won't really change until the whole Establishment changes.'

'Perhaps that's so.' Bobby was so disconcerted by this sophistication of idiom that he managed only the most feeble rejoinder to it. But this passed unremarked, because of an instant and vigorous reaction from Beadon.

'Absolute rot!' Beadon said. 'Change has to begin in the day-rooms and the dorms. My brother says you have to start revolutions on the factory floor.' He turned to Bobby. 'I have two brothers,' he explained politely. 'One's in Chartered Accounting, and the other's in Student Power.'

'I see. Are you in favour of some Student Power at Overcombe?'

'Of course. In all sorts of ways, we're treated like kids in a nursery. Pocket-money shouldn't have to be handed in at the beginning of term.'

'And the books you bring back,' Walcot said, 'shouldn't be censored. Smoking should be legalised.'

'So should beer. English schoolboys used to be brought up on beer. It's in all the old stories, isn't it?' Beadon had appealed to Bobby. 'I think "Legalise Beer" would be a jolly good slogan.'

'It certainly sounds well,' Bobby agreed. 'But do you actually like beer?'

'I haven't tried it, as a matter of fact. In my family, we get a glass of wine on Sundays from the time of our first hols from boarding school.'

'That's terribly civilised.' Bobby felt hopefully that the showing off had begun. 'Do you think it's a good idea,' he asked, 'having those young women in the school, and calling them house-mothers? We just had an old matron.'

'Oh, that!' Beadon was tolerant. 'I don't mind them at all. In fact it's rather jolly having a few birds around.'

'It keeps things normal.' Walcot seemed determined to cap this mature response in his companion. 'There's a man called Freud—have you heard of him?—who says that not mixing up the sexes always is all wrong. Of course, we don't want those girls to play nanny to us. Pulling your ears to see if you've washed behind them, and brushing your hair and tugging your shorts straight.'

'They certainly oughtn't to be allowed in the dorms,' Beadon said.

'Or not in senior dorm.' Walcot offered this by way of judicious qualification. 'It mayn't be too bad an idea for the new bugs. But when you're soon going on to a public school, and get to telling each other what you've heard from your older brothers and so on, it's just not decent having those women snooping around.'

'A man's world,' Beadon said, 'contains a lot that no pure woman should know.'

'For instance, that old Gullible makes you drop your pants for a licking,' Walcot amplified. 'You couldn't tell your mother a thing like that. She might think you wanted to know whether it happened that way in girls' schools too. Which would be absolutely frightful.'

'Yes,' Bobby said—and dimly recalled much speculation of this order. 'But do you mean that the house-mothers get you out of bed in the morning—that sort of thing?'

'They always do that.' Beadon, who appeared to have a cautious streak, was carefully burying the end of his cigarette. 'One oughtn't to complain, I suppose. There may be worse ahead. A prefect with a dog-whip or something.'

'It mayn't quite come to that.' Bobby in his time had been ruthlessly fed with horror-stories by his elder brothers. 'Have you one particular house-mother?'

'Walcot and I have Miss Danbury. She makes us call her Susan. I don't suppose you've seen her, because she wasn't at lunch, She's not altogether bad-looking, as a matter of fact.'

'But what will she be like,' Walcot asked, 'when she's been on the job twenty years? All that asking you about your bowels! It's bound to have a coarsening effect.'

'She may get married,' Bobby said. And he added quickly, 'To one of the masters, for instance.'

'Better dead.' Walcot, for some reason, crossed himself piously. 'You've seen them, haven't you? Gullible gets them cheap.'

'How do you think he manages that? I think there's a regular rate for the job in school-mastering nowadays.'

'Probably not if you've been in gaol,' Beadon said. He spoke without any apparent attempt at producing a witticism. 'And we think that most of them must have been in gaol. It seems to account for things. Overcombe, you know, *is* rather an odd place. Walcot and I are both struck by it. We talk about it quite a lot.'

'That's very interesting.' Bobby was amused by this extraordinary fantasy. 'Of course I agree that a housemother's job must be rather monotonous. Getting you out of bed every blessed morning, and so forth. But don't they ever have a day off? For instance, did Susan get you up on Tuesday morning?'

Even as he uttered this question, Bobby realised it to be fatally deficient in that craft which he had been proposing to summon to his aid. He had meant it to sound so casual that it would receive an answer without remark, and the conversation at once pass on to something else. But it was quite plain that its utter inconsequence had been marked by these sage children at once. And Beadon, at least, had tumbled to the fact that it must hold some ulterior significance. For he was looking very hard at Bobby.

'I don't know, at all,' Beadon said coldly. 'A chap doesn't remember every little thing.'

This was very dreadful. Dishonest fishing after a kind of low-down on Susan was bad enough in itself—but now these boys had detected him in the act. They were realising that this whole encounter had been contrived, and that Old Boy Robert Appleby (scrum-half for England a long time ago) had been chatting them up for some covert purpose of his own. And, of course, their intermingling of sophistication and ignorance was such that they could believe (and presently broadcast) almost anything. They probably knew vaguely about the divorce-courts, and about inquiry-agents who went sniffing about to discover who had been in bed with whom when. They might suppose Susan was implicated in something like that.

It was in the moment of this disaster that there started up in Bobby's mind a notion which (although completely haywire) could conceivably be credited with a certain imaginative audacity. It wasn't possible to tell Beadon and Walcot about the body in the bunker, and about Susan Danbury (not altogether bad-looking) standing (or her double standing?) beside Bobby as he surveyed it. Discretion made this impossible; within half-an-hour the yarn might become the property of the whole school. And some propriety which might equally be called moral or aesthetic made it impossible too. It simply was not conceivable that he should start telling these nice (if variously insufferable) children about a real man found with much of his head shot off in a real bunker on a real golf-course at a real (if obscure) place called Linger. To tell them about this, and to add that their Miss Danbury (whether not altogether bad-looking or not) stood in some ambiguous relationship to plain murder, was a procedure which, quite desperately, was simply not on. And Beadon was now carefully thrusting two or three match-sticks—tokens of the late orgy—into the turf. It was an indication that this unfortunate encounter was over. The rashness of Bobby's eruptive notion can be fairly judged only against the background of this crisis.

'Do you know anything about espionage?' Bobby asked.

'Espionage?' Beadon had repeated the mere sounds phonetically. 'What's that?'

'An old-fashioned word for something that isn't a bit old-fashioned itself.' Bobby managed a short portentous pause. 'I've got to take a risk,' he said. 'You've spotted that there's something funny about me, and I'd better come clean.' He smiled an enigmatic smile. 'By the way, will you both call me Bobby? Or, if you want to be a bit more formal, call me oo8.'

'oo8!' This time, Beadon wasn't at all at sea.

'But don't think I'm a total fraud. I *was* at Overcombe. That's why I've been given this mission.'

'Mission!' Walcot said. Here was something else that rang a bell.

'By M.'

'M?' Walcot's tone told Bobby at once that this last stroke of fantasy had been a little too light-hearted. 'M's in a book,' Walcot said.

'He certainly is.' Bobby managed a chuckle. 'That's why we *call* M. M. After M. in the stories. It amuses him. And he needs what amusement he can get. His is a pretty tough job.'

'Do you mean,' Beadon asked slowly, 'that you're talking about the top man in the Secret Service?'

'Good Lord, no!' By this time, Bobby had managed to suppress a twinge of compunction at thus practising upon the innocence of these infants. 'M. is number two. It's probable that only M. and K. know who the top man is. K. is number three.'

'I see.' Beadon was giving Bobby one of his alarmingly straight looks. 'What you tell us, oo8, is extremely surprising.'

'It is, indeed.' Bobby realised that he was never quite going to know about Beadon. But there was now nothing for it but to press on with the extravagant fabrication he had so rashly embarked upon. 'Of course, Overcombe is rather a surprising place, isn't it? You and Walcot have been clever enough to notice it, although perhaps nobody else has. You've talked to each other about it. Which is why I'm talking to you. You're the only two men who can help. And it's fair to warn you that the going may be pretty sticky.' Bobby waited. It was at least odds on, he told himself, that this heady stuff would carry the day. He was right.

'Go on,' Walcot said in a low voice.

'Wait!' Beadon was suddenly commanding. 'I'm going to make sure we're not being trailed. You can't be too careful. Not at this game.' And Beadon, with a surprising speed, contrived an exit on his stomach from the small hollow in which this remarkable conference had been taking place. Bobby was left wondering just what had brought the word 'game' to his lips. There was, of course, *Kim*, which it was inconceivable that Beadon hadn't read. Kim was the archetype of all Boy Spies. And what Kim had played (against Russian emissaries from across the North-West Frontier) was the Great Game. That must be it.

There was silence for a moment, and then Walcot spoke.

'Tailed,' Walcot said.

'What's that?'

'Beadon should have said "tailed", not "trailed". He hasn't got the vocab right.'

'I suppose not.' Bobby now wondered about the word 'vocab'. Did it, by some faint irony, convey Walcot's knowledge that he was being invited into a world of make-believe? It seemed not possible to tell. In three years' time Messrs Walcot and Beadon, being quite clever, would have entered the No Man's Land of a Lower Sixth. They would be winding up (unless they turned out to be artists of one sort or another—which was unlikely) the life of the imagination, or at least they would be getting it disentangled from that real world in which one progresses to the condition of a Queen's Counsel or Regius Professor or Private Secretary or even Minister of the Crown. But at present— Bobby broke off this useless speculation. Beadon had returned, still on his stomach.

'O.K.,' Beadon said crisply.

'We'll get back to the girl, if you please.' Bobby wasted no time. He had—or he thought he had—lured these boys into a momentary world of make-believe, and he must get such information as he could from them while the illusion held. 'And to Tuesday morning. Was she around?' Bobby felt his own heart-beat foolishly accelerating as he asked this.

'But,' Beadon said, 'just why do you—'

'No questions quite yet, please.' Bobby was very firmly the man close to M. himself. 'And it's vital there should be no mistake. *Was Susan Danbury around?*'

'*Num,*' Walcot said. 'She wasn't around, was she?'

'Or *nonne.*' Beadon chimed in. 'She was around, wasn't she?'

'I learnt all that once—and from somebody who taught Latin rather well.' Bobby, if impatient, was also amused. 'But I'm not saying which answer I want or expect. Just answer this: Was Susan at Overcombe fairly early on Tuesday morning?'

'One has only to have seen her to say she *was*,' Walcot said. 'But one may *not* have seen her, and still be unable to say that she *wasn't*. And we can only say certain things. She didn't come into our dorm at getting-up time.'

'I see.' Bobby felt his fast-beating heart contract. 'And that's wholly unusual? Doesn't she have days off?'

'I don't think anybody's given days off at Overcombe.' Beadon said this sombrely. 'Still, there are mornings when she doesn't come. And Tuesday was one.'

'Somebody else came instead? Another house-mother?'

'I don't think so. No, I can remember that nobody came. You see, there's a bell. It's just that, if Susan doesn't come, you have to jump to the bell, or there may be trouble with some master who's taken it into his head to get up early. You may be sent to run round the cricket-field before breakfast, or something stupid of that kind. You remember the sort of thing.'

'Belsen-and-water,' Walcot said, rather surprisingly. 'That's what a prep school is, wouldn't you say? Of course, a lot more water than Belsen. One has to be fair.'

'Stick to the point, please.' Bobby spoke with the sharpness not of 008 (or 009 or 010) but of M. himself. 'When *did* you see Susan on Tuesday?'

'Not until lunch-time,' Beadon said. 'But that doesn't mean she wasn't at Overcombe. She doesn't teach us, or anything. Other chaps may have seen her. We could ask around. Cautiously, of course.'

'So as not,' Walcot said, 'to arouse a breath of suspicion. You could rely on us.'

Bobby rather doubted it—although he had a feeling that his new assistants might be entirely reliable in other ways. They seemed, for example, to have got the idea of defining precisely the bounds and limitations of their knowledge. And, so far, what he had himself collected was of a negative order. He had no evidence making it impossible that Susan could have been on the golf-course at Linger on Tuesday morning. Between her disappearance there—between *the girl's* disappearance there—and lunch-time at Overcombe it would have been easily possible to drive back to the school. He suddenly realised that what he had wanted the boys to say was that Yes, Susan *had* appeared in their dormitory. In other words, he had been indulging something like a crazy wish himself to be proved mad. Or, if not mad, at least in the grip of a mysterious psychological aberration. Could he be hitching Susan Danbury on to a dream? Had he become a drug addict? He seemed to remember having heard of junkies who had strange fits of amnesia in which they *didn't know* they were junkies. Could that be it? That very solid-seeming Sergeant Howard, for example—might he have been a purely subjective phenomenon? Alternatively, might he be in the middle of a dream now—and never have returned to Over-combe at all? Bobby looked at Beadon and Walcot, and saw that Beadon and Walcot were looking rather curiously at him. They didn't have the appearance of an involuntary manifestation of the unconscious mind during sleep. On the contrary, they simply had the appearance of two school-boys—and of two schoolboys plainly thinking that 008 was behaving strangely. Presumably the disturbing character of his thoughts had resulted in his ceasing to attend to them. But now Beadon was speaking, and with the air of repeating a question which has been ignored.

'Which side is Susan on—theirs or ours? I don't see we can help much, if you won't even tell us that.'

'I'm afraid I don't know.'

'You don't *know*?'

'Definitely not.' Bobby had spoken rather helplessly and at random. But now he saw that, in the kind of environment he had been conjuring up, such a reply would some-times be a perfectly valid one. 'You see,' he added, 'espionage is a very funny thing. There's Intelligence and there's Counter-Intelligence, all mixed up. There are people called double agents. I'm sure you've heard of them. So, quite often, one just doesn't know where one stands. You may be tailing somebody who's really your ally. You simply don't know. And there are rules that don't allow you merely to ask and find out.'

The eyes of Messrs Beadon and Walcot had rounded during these revelations, as they well might. Indeed, it struck Bobby that he had made his point rather well. Moreover, although he had simply invented this vast non-sense about espionage, there was an approximation to truth in what he had said. Cops and Robbers, Goodies and Baddies. He would be unable, upon challenge, to produce a scrap of evidence that Susan didn't stand on the criminal side of the line. Or, for that matter, a scrap of evidence to the contrary.

'It does all tie up,' Beadon was saying. 'Walcot, don't you think?'

Prep schools, Bobby thought, are the most conservative of all educational institutions. Long after public schools have fallen for the modern convention of Christian names, these more juvenile establishments—mere nurseries, as they are—maintain this older and more austere manner of address.

'Yes, it ties up, Beadon.' Walcot glanced at his watch. 'Gosh! Look at the time.'

'Christ!' The assured Beadon was of a sudden comically dismayed. He turned to Bobby. 'I'm sorry, but we damn well have to run for it. Afternoon roll-call is absolutely Gullible's thing. His one bastion against chaos in the day, Mr Hartsilver says.'

'So it is,' Bobby agreed, and stood up. 'I don't half remember it.'

'And I propose to carry an inviolate anatomy through this term. But look—we could meet here again after prep.'

'Very well.' Bobby felt that he couldn't decently expose to the risk of some physical discomfort the persons of Messrs Beadon and Walcot. 'Seven o'clock, is it still? I'll be here. Now, cut along.' They were all three scrambling up towards the avenue. 'But just tell me this. What sort of things tie up?'

'No end of mysterious things.' Beadon had vaulted a fence. 'The Russians, for example.'

'The Russians?'

'Well, the two bearded men who were talking Russian. That right, Walcot?'

'Dead right. And the midnight helicopter.'

'And the man with the missing finger,' Beadon said. 'Don't forget him.'

The boys had vanished, and Bobby—like Shakespeare's Antony—was left alone, whistling to the air. Of the bearded

Russians (but are Russians ever bearded nowadays?) and the midnight helicopter there was a simple, if mortifying, explanation. In appearing to accept Bobby as a mysterious Secret Agent, Beadon and Walcot had merely been having him on. But what about the man with the missing finger? Even if the legend of Bloody Nauze had lingered at Overcombe in a manner which in itself was unlikely enough, what could have prompted Beadon to invoke him in the context he had?

Bobby saw no answer. He also saw that it must be his next business to find one.

CHAPTER SIX

Sir John Appleby, when made aware that any of his children were obscurely at grips with private problems of either an intellectual, a moral, or an emotional sort, had long been in the habit of recommending solitary pedestrianism. If you walk till you drop—he was accustomed to say—it is at least possible that something sensible will come into your head during the last half-mile. If you simply retire to your own room, shove your backside into an excessively sprung easy-chair, and there grimly cerebrate, the chances are that you will eventually do no more than crawl into bed—to wake up six to eight hours later with an unsolved conundrum and a filthy headache.

Bobby Appleby had put in a good many years resenting and resisting Boy-Scout wisdom of this sort. So it must have been for entirely independent reasons that he had in fact taken to covering the countryside with a long stride whenever there was something to think out. He did this now. To the north of Overcombe ran a skyline of downland intriguingly humped and nicked by human hands a very long time ago. These tumuli, barrows, vallums and the like had been, in the way of sheer trudge, a considerable challenge to the energies of small boys. But the cheerfully anarchic life of Overcombe (with, as Bobby had remembered, that late-afternoon roll-call as its only effectively fixed point) had admitted excursions, licit or illicit, of quite an ambitious sort. Bobby had come to know the Ridgeway rather well.

He made for it as soon as Beadon and Walcot had scampered off. On Lark Hill he surveyed the Linchets— monuments to the laborious husbandry of goodness-knew-whom. From Bleak Barn (he remembered it had been called that on the Ordnance Survey map sent him by his mother) he contemplated anew the surprisingly indelicate Long Man. To this figure in the chalk (the erection of an ancient people, as it had been cryptically described to him by a sophisticated contemporary infant) he had owed the comforting knowledge that he was not the unique victim of some mysterious physiological malady. Into the great British camp beyond it, a kind of Olympic Stadium for the Games of a giant race, he didn't now go, but he walked on as far as the Great Smithy before dropping down into the valley once more. The Great Smithy seemed to have been much tidied up by the Ministry of Works. Its narrow entrance, although dark as ever and threateningly flanked by the same huge sarsen stones, was now approached by a narrow brick path, and the mound of turf over the pre-historic barrow which the Smithy in fact was might have been shaved by a lawn-mower scaled up to the general proportions of the scene. But the beech-trees still shadowed it in their dark clumps. It was still a lonely and eerie place. Once it had even been frightening.

And now—Bobby told himself as he turned away—it was quite possible that he had seen it for the last time.

His walk had brought him not much more than the ghost of an idea. He had rejected the impulse to ring up home and report. He had turned down as inadvisable for the present the prompting to shove in on Susan Danbury again and have it out with her. But he had remembered one of the customs of Overcombe which was quite likely still to obtain. Evening prep was taken either by a single victimised and fidgety master, or by an infant grandly known as Prefect of Studies—who in theory was armed for the duration of these occasions with disciplinary powers of the lines-awarding order. But nobody much attended to the Prefect of Studies—who had commonly learnt from experience anyway that his companions had their own disciplinary resources should his conduct of affairs be judged objectionable. He could be well booted, for example, during some convenient game. In an extreme case, he could simply be scragged on the spot—while Dr Gulliver and Mr Onslow were enjoying in their own apartments a dignified repose, and before the junior staff had returned from the Leather Bottle.

It must be one of the few alleviations in the lot of the Doctor's assistants, Bobby reflected, that the nearest human habitation to Overcombe was a pub. The staff commonly contrived to get there by opening time, and to spend in the bar a comfortable hour fortifying themselves against the remaining harassments of the fag-end of the day. Bobby's ghost of an idea was simply to join them there. They were probably quite vague about the movements and occasions of Gulliver's lunchtime visitor, and it might be possible to pick up something from them in the way of gossip. Bobby, of course, had never in his juniority entered the Leather Bottle, and the comportment of the daily Overcombe contingent there was necessarily a matter of conjecture. But it seemed reasonable to suppose a more or less unbuttoned mood obtained.

Bobby glanced at his watch, and calculated that he had a quarter of an hour in hand. Not wanting to find himself hanging round the Leather Bottle before that modest pothouse opened its doors, he decided to linger for a little where he was. It was an agreeably lonely situation. He had been dropping down a winding track between high turf-covered banks, in a late-afternoon air which was still warm and murmurous with insects. But just over the bank to his left it would be warmer still, and there would be a whole landscape to survey beneath the westering sun. Perhaps the contemplation of this would give his thoughts some nudge. Bobby scrambled over the bank, and sat down on the fine grass which here sprang everywhere from the chalk. There was a flock of sheep in the middle-distance and a kestrel overhead. A minute or two before, he had been listening to the song of a lark. But the lark had fallen silent, and now there wasn't a sound. Only there was. For suddenly Bobby was hearing voices from somewhere on the path down which he had come. And they had barely become distinguishable before Bobby was on his feet again, oddly alert. Within seconds he knew that, however unaccountable his reaction, his ears had not deceived him. He was listening to men's voices, speaking in a foreign tongue.

It wasn't French—or any other language with Latin in its ancestry. It wasn't German. Perhaps it was Swedish, Danish—something like that. Or perhaps—

There didn't come into Bobby's head any notion of lying low, or of otherwise wasting time. He reached the top of the bank—a commanding position—in a bound. The men —there were two of them—had come abreast of him, and their heads were on a level with his feet.

'Good afternoon,' Bobby said.

The men came to a halt. It was not entirely the natural thing to do—except, of course, that Bobby's appearance had been sudden and perhaps surprising. Wayfarers when saluted by other and momentarily pausing wayfarers commonly deliver their own greetings while continuing in motion. Halt, and something further has to be said—an exchange of conjectures about the weather, or about the lie of the land, or the mileage to this place or that. But neither of the two men appeared momentarily to have anything to say. If they had stopped other than in a purely involuntary fashion it had been to look at Bobby rather hard. And Bobby looked hard at them. They were both bearded men. And both had haircuts of a very close-clipped sort.

Bobby found he didn't care for this. The reaction was perhaps illiberable in him, since he was himself clean-shaven and given to wearing his hair somewhat notably long. But it wasn't the aesthetics of the situation that much compelled him now. Rather it was the topography. For he couldn't at all see where these industriously conversing foreigners had come from. Of course they had been invisible to him when behind him on the narrow sunken track. And he must have been invisible to them. But the track had snuggled between its banks only a hundred yards or so below the Great Smithy. And all around was the bare down. Bobby found himself scanning the down for abandoned parachutes, and then—without intending anything dramatic—equally scanning the heavens for, perhaps, a drifting balloon. For everywhere a great silence reigned.

The bearded men remarked this behaviour. One of them even imitated it.

'Good afternoon,' this man said. 'Beautifully still. Very little wind. Nice walking weather.'

'So unspoilt a countryside,' the second man said. He continued simply to look at Bobby. 'And yet the urban centres are not far distant, after all. It is sad that people are so unaware of their rural heritage.'

'Yes,' Bobby said. Both men spoke very good English. But there was surely something a little odd about what they offered by way of chat. And there was something odd about their clothes as well. Or was there? Bobby found that he was merely thinking they weren't dressed as they ought to be. They were dressed rather as he was. But they were chunky men—there was no other way of describing them—and what they *should* have been wearing was suits with chunky double-breasted jackets together with rather formal Homburg hats. For the world they belonged to was the world he had been conjuring up for Beadon and Walcot—and which Beadon and Walcot had so promptly and obligingly peopled with two bearded Russians. These men, in fact, *were* the boys' bearded Russians. Bobby was very properly disturbed by this weird conclusion. There seemed no way of escaping it, all the same.

And now—even as Bobby was obliged to acknowledge something incredible violently tugging at his mind—the silence of outer nature was broken. For a moment he thought that it was the buzzing of an insect quite close to his ear. Then his glance was drawn to Moby Dick. Moby Dick was a spinney, and from Overcombe it appeared as a wedge-shaped object lying on the horizon of the down. Hence its name—although it looked like a black whale rather than a white one. Something like an insect, or rather something like a dragonfly, was just disappearing over Moby Dick. A momentary change in such light breeze as there was had brought its tiny buzz, or rather its tiny clatter, this way. The dragonfly was a helicopter. It vanished before Bobby could begin to estimate its line of flight. It might have come from any quarter of the horizon.

The two men had also caught sight of the stumpy little aerial argosy. They didn't look too pleased with it. For that matter, they hadn't been looking too pleased with Bobby either. And now Bobby wondered to what extent he had given himself away as a young man desperately groping after some sense of what he was up against. But perhaps it wasn't like that at all. Perhaps the bearded men were unaware of anything that could be called suspicion as being directed upon them. They were doing nothing more out of the way than taking an ordinary sort of walk in this rather lonely place, and they had done no more than show themselves as slightly taken aback when someone had suddenly bounced up on a grassy bank and addressed them.

But—Bobby asked himself—if the two strangers were not in the least possessed by any sense of crisis, why was he himself gripped by precisely that? For what was upon him was not merely a feeling of hovering revelation. His whole body was tensed for action—much as if he was on his toes behind his scrum, well inside his opponents twenty-five, while trailing by three points during the last minutes of the game. But, no—it wasn't even quite like that. What he was vividly aware of was *danger*. Yet neither of these men had made the slightest movement of a muscle which could be construed as a threat. Unless he was imagining things—which was likely enough—it could only be that he had stood in momentary telepathic communication with something going on inside their heads.

They were moving on. They were moving on—Bobby's sharpened sense told him—fractionally more slowly than they had been walking before. One tends to do this when anxious to obviate the suspicion that one is retreating in disorder. They were two innocent wayfarers, with plenty of leisure before them, going on their way after a casual encounter in this peaceful spot. One of them had even wished Bobby a good-afternoon—a somewhat formal thing to do, but then foreigners are like that. The other had displayed a splendid set of teeth in an obtrusive style. And now their chunky figures were already diminishing down the path.

Bobby found that he had sat down abruptly on a tump of grass. His body, he supposed, had to cope with the excess of adrenalin, or whatever it was, that this real or imagined crisis had summoned into his blood-stream. In any case, there was no point in following these two men. He would do much better to manage some thinking about them, and about the whole transformed face—if it *was* transformed—of the quest he had embarked upon.

Beadon had spoken of bearded Russians, and bearded Russians had appeared. Walcot had offered a midnight helicopter, and a helicopter had presented itself in the afternoon sky. There need be nothing in this—absolutely nothing at all. If a couple of foreigners were around, they were around: it was as simple as that. And helicopters potter about the heavens by night as by day. Messrs Beadon and Walcot had produced these appearances as mysterious only—one might say—upon challenge. With the dead man in the bunker, with the mystery of Susan Danbury, these things need have nothing to do.

But Beadon had mentioned the dead man in the bunker as well. Or at least he had mentioned—and again as mysterious—'the man with the missing finger'. Bobby saw, clearly and too late, that he ought not to have let Dr Gulliver's afternoon roll-call abrupt whatever further communication the boys had to make. When you are dealing with something as desperate as murder, you ought not to hold up your investigations just to spare a couple of tough little creatures the risk of a mild ritual licking. But for the moment Beadon and Walcot were beyond Bobby's ken. He couldn't simply march straight back to the school and demand instant access to them—or not without what might be a rashly obtrusive scene. They would turn up again as they had promised, no doubt. Meanwhile, he must make some other cast. The Leather Bottle, after all, must remain next on his list.

Bobby got to his feet, and then firmly sat down again. It seemed to be his impulse to rush around. And that was all wrong. You don't plant the ball firmly between the posts by puffing and panting and pounding all over the place. You stay poised on your toes at least for those fractions of a second in which you can take in the field and think something out.

Why had the Russians and the helicopter (and, for that matter, the man with the missing finger) been conjured into being by Beadon and Walcot amid that aroma of Turkish tobacco? Entirely because Bobby had invented for himself a role in a spy story. And why had he done *that*? Superficially, it had been to catch the interest and gain the help of a couple of schoolboys who might have been bored or puzzled or offended by the obscure situation which Bobby was actually involved with. Yet it had been an utterly spontaneous and uncalculating thing. 'Do you know anything about espionage?' Bobby had suddenly asked—and had then been constrained to go on to a great deal of rot about M. (and N. and K.) and 008. He hadn't even been at all sure that Beadon and Walcot believed a word of it. Indeed, hadn't the belief been, in an utterly obscure and unaccountable way, all on his own part? Hadn't it sprung from something almost wholly bizarre which had just hovered on the farthest verge of his consciousness when Hartsilver had given him a little fresh information about Bloody Nauze?

Bobby looked at his watch. The Leather Bottle would be open by now, and by the time he reached it the employees of Dr Gulliver and Mr Onslow would be well into their first gin-and-tonic or their first pint. Which would be all to the good, no doubt.

The exterior of the Leather Bottle certainly hadn't changed, except that a discouraged-looking placard outside its only entrance intimated a willingness to purvey grills, snacks at the bar, freshly-cut sandwiches (since there are, of course, other sorts) and morning coffee. The morning coffee, Bobby thought, was the most incredible of the lot; it was inconceivable that it should be made in such a place, let alone called for and consumed. What the beer would be like, he didn't know at all; he resolved to look round until he spotted an unopened bottle of reputable whisky, and firmly ask for that. There was a possibility that his visit would be abortive. The people at Overcombe nowadays might have the habit of piling into their cars and going somewhere a little more gay. And it was too early for any locals, so there was no chance of useful gossip from them. That would leave only the pub-keeper or the barmaid. Real detectives, he knew, possessed an advanced technique for eliciting information from people of that sort. It was something he had never been required to have a go at.

In the poky entrance it would have been possible to shove open the doors of the saloon bar and the public bar simultaneously with your two elbows. There was no sound of revelry to guide him either way, so he tried the saloon bar first. It was unoccupied except by a lot of flies, and they were all buzzing at a window-pane in an effort to get out. The only decoration was an uncertain sketch of the Great Smithy, done direct on a decaying wallpaper. Some strolling artist had no doubt executed this on a basis of so many pints to the square yard. Bobby turned back and tried the public bar. This too was without patrons, which was discouraging. But the landlord—as he should presumably be called—was in attendance, and beguiling vacancy by filling in a football coupon. Perhaps he had been much busier earlier in the day. He hadn't shaved.

'Good evening,' Bobby said, and approached the bar. To do so he had to negotiate two one-armed bandits and a juke-box. Bobby thought poorly of these. One could play darts, he saw—but there was no shove-halfpenny board, let alone bar billiards. Perhaps he could challenge the landlord to a game of darts, and so get chatty with him that way. He didn't seem a very naturally chatty sort. His response to Bobby's greeting had simply been to put down his assault on the Pools with visible reluctance and favour his customer with a gloomy stare. At the risk of some gastronomic discomfort, Bobby decided to abandon the quest for an unopened whisky-bottle and make a bold bid for favour. 'Pint of best bitter, please,' he said cheerfully.

Socially, this didn't appear to be a particular success. The landlord went through the required motions in silence, picked up his coupon again, wetted the point of a pencil in a dribble of beer on the counter, and added a further prognostication to his list.

'People from the school come in here often nowadays?'

Bobby asked. He received in reply no more than an indeterminate motion of the head. 'The fact is,' Bobby said, 'that I'd like to know something about the place. I'm thinking of sending my kid there.'

'Huh!' The landlord had at last uttered. 'Entered at birth, is it? Eton and 'arrow stuff.' He sniffed with overt contempt.

'Not birth at all. The kid's eight tomorrow. That's why I've come down.'

'Eight tomorrow!' The landlord stared at Bobby. ''ere, mister, 'ow old are you?'

'Twenty-four. But that's tomorrow too. Timothy and I have the same birthday.'

'Been living it up quite some time, 'aven't you?' The landlord was now staring at Bobby with proper respect. 'Learnt your way about early, it seems to me.'

'I was born in India, you see.' Bobby spoke modestly. 'A hot climate. It makes a difference.'

'It can't be 'ealthy, that can't. Worn out before your time, you'll be. Mark my words.'

'Well, I'm quite O.K. now, thanks.' Bobby raised his glass of beer affably, and at the same time contrived what he hoped was an atrociously vulgar wink. 'And keep my eyes open as I move around. Some nice pieces they have, up at that school. Unexpected in a place like that. Housemothers, they call them. I'd call them—'

'Har-har!' Unexpected raucous laughter from the landlord relieved Bobby of the necessity of concluding this coarse pleasantry. 'Quite in your Timothy's line soon—eh? —if 'e's 'is father's son. But one of them girls comes in here regular. Name of Susan. And I wouldn't 'arf mind.'

'Won't you have something on me?' Bobby asked. It was clear to him that only an aggressive and forward policy would enable him to carry on this revolting conversation. Even before the mention of Susan's name it had been pretty thick.

'I don't mind if I 'ave a drop with bitters—not at this hour.' The landlord spoke quite affably as he reached for a bottle of gin. 'Susan,' he repeated. 'Name of Susan. I'd rather 'ave 'er than a square meal any day. And there's not many as you can say that of.'

'That's a true word.' Bobby put his beer down on a ledge beneath the bar. He was pretty sure he couldn't drink another drop of it.

'Only her tastes are peculiar, if you ask me. Not keen to show the youngsters a bit of life, the same that Timothy's mother seems to have been. This Susan comes in 'ere to meet an ol' man, more often than not. An ol' man 'e is from the school too—which is another peculiar thing to my mind. Name of 'artsilver.'

'Hartsilver!'

'The drawering-master, 'e's said to be. A low class of employment. But this girl comes in to meet him quiet-like. More private than up at the school, I suppose. And I'll tell you another thing. Sometimes there's a young chap as well. Appears from nowhere, 'e does. Not a local. Might have dropped from the clouds. They go into the garden, they do, and don't know I've sometimes watched them through that there key-'ole.' The landlord pointed unblushingly. 'And they're that much in an 'uddle, they might as well be all three beneath the same blanket. I don't like it—not in a respectable 'ouse like this.'

'You mean—' Bobby stared at the landlord aghast.

'Well, no. That's only by way of passing a joke, you might say. You learn the uses of 'armless 'umour in a job like mine. But very thick about *something*, they are. Very thick, indeed. 'Ere—where's your beer?'

Bobby retrieved his beer hastily, but was fortunately not constrained to apply himself to it. For now a diversion occurred. The door of the public bar had opened—had in fact been kicked open—to admit two young men. Bobby glanced at them and recognised them instantly as among those grown-ups privileged to partake of Dr Gulliver's nutritious midday meal. There was to be a contingent from Overcombe at the Leather Bottle after all.

'Good evening, gentlemen. The usual, I suppose?' It seemed to be the landlord's policy to make a considerable effort of cordiality towards regulars from Overcombe.

'The bloody usual twice, George.' The first young man—the one who had kicked open the door—looked round the bar disgustedly. '*Pas de jupe,*' he said. '*Aucun oiseau. Bloody hell.*'

'But, Jakin, we ought to have invited them, don't you think?' Unlike the first young man, who was beefy and choleric, the second young man was pale and mild. 'You can't expect the girls to come in a lot on their own.'

'Rot, Lew. The new one does, if George is to be believed. But perhaps you're right. Perhaps they don't care to drop in with strange types lurking around.' The young man called Jakin glowered at Bobby. Disappointment in the expectation of eligible female society had put him in a bad temper. He had raised his voice as he spoke, and now he raised it further. 'Bet you a fiver,' he said, 'I lay her before the end of term.'

'Shut up, Jakin.' Lew appeared to feel a certain measure of impropriety in his companion's remarks. 'Stick your mug in your pot, and pipe down.'

'Do you take me on, or don't you? A fiver that I lay the Danbury—'

Jakin broke off—surprised, and perhaps even alarmed, that the strange type was advancing upon him in long strides across the bar. Half-way, however, the strange type checked himself, assumed an expression of elaborate unconcern, felt in a trouser-pocket for sixpence and veered off in the direction of one of the one-armed bandits. Sir John Appleby, had he been present on this interesting occasion, might not have been able to award his son high marks for technique. But he would undoubtedly have awarded him very high marks indeed for self-control.

Bobby shoved sixpence in the idiotic machine and pulled the handle. The machine went through its routine performance—one calculated to suggest to the folk-mind a high complexity of shifting and changing chances. Unfortunately the machine also judged it impressive to make a good deal of noise, so that for some seconds he had lost the opportunity further to edify himself by Jakin's conversation. He hoped it would occur to neither of the young men to put a coin in the juke-box. That would reduce the possibility of further successful eavesdropping to about zero. It was odd that neither young man seemed aware of having seen him before. But Jakin had clearly registered him only as an objectionable foreign body of a generalised sort. Bobby wasn't so clear about Lew, who was possibly a slightly more cerebral type.

The one-armed bandit had, of course, yielded no dividend. Bobby produced another sixpence, but held on to it parsimoniously while affecting to study with concentration the creature's gaudy dial. Like the waiter in Mr Eliot's quaint poem, it was prolific in oranges, bananas, figs and hothouse grapes. Hence, no doubt, the alternative name of fruit-machine. Or had the manufacturers gone fruity because, for some extraneous reason, the term had already been applied to their contraptions? Bobby dismissed this irrelevant speculation as he heard Jakin speaking once more.

'Herself to herself,' he was saying. 'That's our Susan. Been at Overcombe eight weeks now, and what do you know? Not so much as if she's ever been there.'

'Been there?' Lew asked.

'You know bloody well where. And yet she's a beddable bitch. I've watched her with the other drabs. Definitely not Lesbian.'

Bobby, although the blood was behaving awkwardly

in his temples and before his inner eye invitingly hovered a vision of Jakin flat on the floor with a badly bruised jaw, concentrated doggedly on the serious business of the day. It hadn't occurred to him—nor had the talk of Beadon and Walcot suggested—that Susan was quite a new arrival at Overcombe. There had been her manner with Hartsilver, for example, when she had come into his hut. That had somehow suggested a more established relationship than would normally develop in the inside of a term.

'Would you say she was a trained nurse?' Lew was asking. 'She seemed to be always in and out of the San. when that pal of Gulliver's was supposed to be recuperating there.'

'Recuperating?' Jakin asked.

'Convalescing, or whatever.'

'*Supposed* to be?'

'Well, there was something odd about it, wasn't there?' As he asked this question, Lew looked quite acute. Bobby made a motion as if about to put his second sixpence in the machine, and then paused again in profound study of its obscure symbolism. 'Do you know that one day they brought him into the Upper Third and said he was going to teach Latin? But it didn't work, and they took him away again.' Lew paused for a swig at his tankard. 'And now he's vanished without a word spoken.'

'Nut case, wasn't he?' Jakin was contemptuous. 'A by-blow of Gulliver's if you ask me, and gone off his rocker. Now they've had to shove him in the bin. Did you ever get a good look at him?'

'Not really. But I noticed he had a finger missing.'

'A screw loose and a finger missing.' Jakin appeared to find this witticism highly entertaining. 'Have you come across anybody who knew anything about him?'

'Nobody at all.' Lew again consulted his tankard, and then glanced curiously in Bobby's direction. This con-strained Bobby to operate the bandit again, with the result that he missed out on something. When the clatter of the machine had subsided again, Jakin was speaking.

'A photograph?' Jakin said.

'One of those group affairs. There's a pile of them in a drawer in common room. This one was about twelve years' back. And there was this chap uncommonly like Gulliver's mysterious guest.'

'To hell with him, anyway. This is a damned dull pub. What about a game of darts?'

'No time.' Lew had looked at his watch. 'Back to the nick, old boy.' Quite unexpectedly, Lew swung round on Bobby. 'I think,' he asked politely, 'that you were lunching at Overcombe today, sir?'

'Yes, I was.' Bobby found himself quite taken aback by this civilised conduct on Lew's part.

'Gent come to see after the school for 'is kid,' the landlord struck in informatively. 'An eight-year-old, 'e 'as. And if you knew 'is own age, you'd be surprised.'

Bobby remembered with alarm the absurd story he had told about himself. He didn't feel he at all wanted the ribaldry of Jakin directed on it. Not that it hadn't been ribald in itself. It might give Susan a very bad impression of him, if it got around.

'I was at Overcombe myself,' he said hastily. 'About a dozen years ago. I suppose you haven't been teaching there very long?'

'Six terms—the same as Jakin.' Lew, although he had moved towards the door, appeared willing to converse. 'The pay's lousy at a prep school, but the work's not too bad.'

'The work's damn all.' Jakin struck a more robust note. 'Keep on the right side of the little brutes—don't expect them to learn anything, or rubbish of that sort—and they leave you more or less alone. Of course the terms are a bit long. Twelve weeks. Half as long again as at Oxford. I'm an Oxford man.'

'Is that so?' Bobby was beginning to feel almost a professional interest in Jakin; this was one of the occasions upon which he obscurely felt it a pity that one isn't really allowed to put characters into the *nouvelle écriture*. 'F.L.'s an Oxford man,' he said. 'And a Cambridge man too. And Yale. And played for both sides in the Eton and Harrow match.'

This ancient Overcombe joke went down well. The Oxford man (Bobby had never before heard anyone announce, *tout court*, that he was an Oxford man) roared with laughter. Lew, perhaps a Cambridge man, laughed less unrestrainedly. Bobby wondered whether he could briefly detain these two devoted pedagogues over another drink. They had already been uncommonly informative without his so much as uttering. Under judicious questioning, they might—even quite unconsciously—reveal a great deal more. The trouble was that Bobby didn't have very clearly in his head what questions he wanted to ask. In the last ten minutes the outlines of his problem had shifted sharply, and he wasn't at all sure what sort of picture he was staring at.

Susan Danbury must be counted as practically a New Girl at Overcombe. She was mysteriously thick with Hartsilver. Bloody Nauze had been back at Overcombe recently, apparently as some sort of invalid friend of Gulliver's. Susan had been mysteriously thick with him too. Hartsilver must have *known* it was Nauze; along with Gulliver and Onslow, he was probably the only person left at Overcombe who *would* know. But Hartsilver, who appeared to be the soul of openness and simplicity, had concealed this knowledge from Bobby. More than that, he had put on an astonishing piece of play-acting when confronted by Bobby's quest for Nauze. Recalling this now, Bobby simply felt that it took his breath away. One just didn't know where one stood in a world in which poor old Hartsilver, failed artist, was minded to behave like that.

Nauze had been a patient in the school sick-room, with Susan trotting in and out on him. And then—most perplexing scrap of information of all—there had been some abortive attempt to get him to teach Latin—to do again what he had once done superbly well. What on earth could that have been in aid of? Could it simply have proceeded from a feeling of Gulliver's that his guest (or patient) ought to do a bit to earn his keep? Whatever had been the idea, it hadn't worked. 'They took him away again.' These had been Lew's exact words. Bobby stared at them inside his own head—and as he did so they became immensely significant. They carried an implication of guardianship—something like that. 'A nut case,' had been Jakin's immediate comment. That was it. Nauze had come to Overcombe, or been brought to Overcombe, as the consequence of some sort of nervous breakdown. He had come to be *cured*. He had come, say, to be patched up to a point at which he could again—gym-shoe in hand—confront a dozen small boys with *mensa* and *amo*; conduct the very cleverest of them to the knowledge that *Gallia est omnis divisa in partes tres*. And the therapy hadn't worked. It hadn't worked at all. Nauze was now dead.

Gulliver had been blank about Nauze. Onslow had been blank about Nauze. Hartsilver, perhaps with greater cunning, had been communicative about Nauze and successfully blank as well. As for the girl, she had been very blank indeed. Bobby had confronted her—his turning up had confronted her—with a situation (it had been possible to feel) which she had barely been able to control. She had managed what now struck him as having had something of the character of a holding operation. And she had walked away on it.

Suicide. When people were confronted, within their own circle, with some particularly ghastly suicide it was surely their instinct to keep mum. Could Bloody Nauze conceivably have committed suicide? Was it possible to imagine a man doing just *that* to ... to his own head? Bobby shivered. But there had been no sign of a weapon. Could he have fallen on top of it? But then? The body vanishing, and now all this maze of deception and lies! Suicide didn't make sense. Add the Russians, and even the helicopter if you pleased, and it made less sense still.

But what to ask Messrs Jakin and Lew? This was the immediate problem—and Bobby shelved it by saying something hospitable about a quick one. Messrs Jakin and Lew, moments before so urgently cognizant of a need to return to the service of education, seemed not disposed to resist this. Bobby, after proper consultation, called for three large brandies. It wasn't quite his notion of something to gulp down an hour before dinner-time. But Jakin and Lew appeared to have no doubts about what to drink when the cost was on someone else.

It still wasn't very clear to Bobby what further line he should take, and he found himself seeking inspiration in the spectacle of external nature. In other words, he found himself gazing between the heads of Jakin and Lew, and through the only window of the public bar. It was in a very special guise, however, that external nature met his regard. In fact, it was in the guise of Susan Danbury. She was looking straight at him, and it was evident that she saw him clearly. She raised a hand, put it to her lips. She raised it further, and beckoned.

Part Three

SIR JOHN APPLEBY

CHAPTER SEVEN

IT WAS PROBABLE, Appleby told himself, that Bobby would not be heard of until he had something positive to report. So there was nothing surprising in his not having rung up the previous night. He hadn't left Dream until the early afternoon. If his destination was Overcombe (and Appleby was pretty sure it was) he would almost certainly have put up somewhere near the school, and thus have established a base for operations. It was only today, Friday, that he would really be on the job.

Appleby finished his breakfast, and picked up *The Times*. At their moonlight meeting the night before, Sergeant Howard had told him that—against Howard's own inclination—the mystery of the bunker had got into at least one of the evening papers. It was a story with the makings of mild sensation, and there would certainly be more about it in the dailies this morning. Not, perhaps, anything that could be called additional hard news—but at least a repeat of yesterday's report, with some vague speculation thrown in.

The Times yielded nothing at all: Appleby went through it twice to make quite sure of the fact. No doubt it had held its hand, he concluded, over what might still be interpreted as a trivial prank. But this would not hold off the press as a whole. The mere fact that the young man who had claimed to find a dead body was the son of a retired Police Commissioner would make news of a sort in itself. Appleby tried the two other morning papers regularly delivered at Dream—one chiefly for the reason that it carried a strip-cartoon of what Judith considered to be rather an endearing dog. There was nothing in either of them. The mysterious affair at Linger had dropped abruptly out of the news.

Appleby's initial reaction was to feel relieved. He had no fancy for Applebys figuring in crime-reports. And, of course, things *did* just drop out of the news. Quite big things sometimes did just that. Here or there about the globe the world was at last plainly coming to an end; there would be columns and columns about events presaging crisis, genocide, universal disaster; and then this would vanish away with a ruthless abruptness to make room for something else of the same sort. It wasn't exactly suppression. It was just a hunch among those controlling what Bobby called the mass media that people would rather have something new.

But these considerations scarcely applied to this sudden treating of the obscure little affair of the bunker as what Bobby—once more—would call a non-event. Or perhaps an anti-happening, Appleby told himself as he strolled out into the garden.

The lawn seemed to be littered with dead birds, as if some band of marksmen had turned up at dawn and conducted a hideous *battue*. That happened long before midsummer, if you had poplars: twigs and leaves of a blackened silver came tumbling down and around at every breeze. Solo Hoobin was ambling up and down with an effect of the largest leisure, propelling a contraption which was supposed to gather up this litter into a bag. The aged Hoobin had not yet presented himself for his day's labour; he was no doubt still engaged in vindicating his character as a perusing man by reading a chapter of *Deuteronomy* or *Leviticus*—occupation which, as being of a devotional order, it would be profane and impious in his employer to endeavour to abridge.

Solo Hoobin, Appleby recalled, was regarded by his venerable uncle as not yet wench-high. But it was only in a figurative sense that this held true. Solo had been crouched over his machine; now he had removed its bag, straightened up, and pitched its contents approximately in the direction of a wheelbarrow designed to receive them. Solo was quite as tall as Bobby, and his hair was even longer. Appleby was never quite sure whether Solo wore Bobby's cast-off jeans, or Bobby wore Solo's. Not that you could mistake the one for the other, for whereas Bobby grew more or less steadily broader as your eye moved from his feet upwards, with Solo it was the other way round. In an obscure fashion they got on rather well together, just as Appleby, equally oddly, got on rather well with Solo's often infuriating uncle. It wasn't that the two youths had grown up together in a kind of feudal relationship. Solo was half a dozen years younger than Bobby, and had been imported to Dream only quite recently as some sort of prop to Hoobin Senior in his declining years. It was just that they seemed rather to like each other.

This train of reflection did no more than pass over the surface of Appleby's mind. It was what prompted him, nevertheless, to pause and have a word with the modestly industrious Solo now. He might very easily have walked past with no more than a good-morning. The circumstance was one which Appleby was to reflect on afterwards in a mood of some sobriety.

'And how is the moped going, Solo?' Appleby asked. It was only lately that Solo, who appeared to be of a thrifty disposition, had acquired one of these unambitious conveyances. Appleby suspected that Bobby—for whom Solo cleaned golf-clubs, whitened tennis-shoes, made emergency trips to Linger post office with important manuscripts and the like—had put up the last ten pounds or so necessary for the purchase. The aged Hoobin had disapproved, and Appleby himself had felt misgivings. But Solo—although never quite all there, and decidedly less than all there at the full of the moon—commanded almost preternaturally

swift reaction times, and it seemed reasonably probable
that he would survive the acquisition of an internal com-
bustion engine. Hoobin Senior abounded in predictions
that his nephew would presently be maimed and lamed for
life. But then Hoobin Senior made the same prediction
(with a superadded glee) whenever Appleby himself was
prompted to display his skill with a scythe or a chain-saw.
'Are you thinking of taking your test with it yet?' Appleby
pursued. Appleby had a professional faith in the importance of driving-tests, licences and general regimentation—
or so his family unkindly alleged. So he didn't want Solo
to spend an unconcerned lifetime behind an L-plate.

'Urr,' Solo said, and ran a hand through his unkempt
locks. Solo had considerable skill in answering inconvenient questions with the appearance of having been deprived
by an ungenerous Nature of the divine faculty of articulate
speech.

'Have you been for any long trips lately?' Appleby pursued—this by way of producing a more congenial topic.

'Lunnon,' Solo said. 'Been to Lunnon.'

Appleby remembered that the moon *was* at the full;
that it was under its brilliant illumination, indeed, that
he had met and conversed with Sergeant Howard on the
golf-course. Solo's persuasion that he had, whether by one
means or another, visited this mysterious metropolis was
a regular feature of what must be called his manic phase.

'London?' Appleby repeated. 'Well, I used to live there
myself.' This was an evasive remark. It seemed immoral
to acquiesce in Solo's delusions, and at the same time un-
kind not to accept them.

'Great orchards there were everywhere,' Solo said. 'And
the paths atween them paved with gold.' He paused re-
flectively. 'But,' he added, 'rabbits be scarce there.'

'There aren't so many as there once were.' Appleby saw
a route to saner ground. 'Where have you been going for
your rabbits lately, Solo?'

'Gold-course,' Solo said. 'Wi' Jem Puckrup. Jem ha' ferret.'

'Ah, yes. Well, it can't be called poaching, I think. Rabbits are only a nuisance on a golf-course.' Appleby was about to move on, but was prompted to ask another question. 'When were you there last, Solo?'

'Urr.' Solo had to think. 'Monday night, it 'twere. Jem and me slep' there.'

Appleby stared at Solo. He was wondering whether he ought to be at all surprised by this casually tendered information. When the aged Hoobin, in the presence of his nephew, had ghoulishly discussed the probability of unknown horrors on the golf course on Monday night, Solo had displayed not the slightest interest in the subject. He had merely doodled with his sickle on the drive. Of course the Linger golf-course was a large area, and there was very little reason to suppose that the slumbers of Solo and his friend Jem had been disturbed by anything untoward there. But it wasn't exactly a matter to let pass unexamined.

'How many rabbits, Solo?' It was necessary to remember that Solo, like other wild creatures, was easily alarmed. And Solo's wildness, or at least his closeness to a primeval state, was never to be forgotten. Solo's mother, a dark little woman, had been a Bunn, and it was well known that the Bunns had retired to the deep woodland towards the end of the Celtic Iron Age and seldom shown up since. Solo's mother must have been captured by a Saxon Hoobin during a foray of comparatively recent date. Solo, emerging from childhood, had been turned into somebody's garden boy, and broken to his tasks with some severity. That he continued to work after a fashion at Dream (where even his venerable uncle was forbidden to take a strap to him) might be attributed to the softening power of kindness, or it might just be a matter of reflexes. But Solo was still liable, metaphorically at least, to make for his ancestral silvan fastnesses when scared.

125

'Two,' Solo said. 'Four.' He performed some complicated ritual of numeration with his fingers. 'Five rabbits come first light Tuesday.'

'And then you came straight home?'

'Not till Jem and me were clemmed. Then we came home-along.'

'I see.' Appleby did his best to impart a casual air to this untoward exhibition of curiosity on his own part. Not that he felt it was much good. Deep beneath Solo's sluggish and straying conscious mind lay intuitive perceptions which were very acute indeed. It was certain that these were alerted now. 'You waited till you felt hungry, Solo, before coming back to Dream. And you had your breakfast and then turned up to work. You must have bolted it. For you were well on time.'

'Urr.' Solo perhaps intended a gracious acknowledgement of this commendation from his employer. 'Afore uncle, I were.'

'Solo, are you sure you and Jem Puckrup didn't see anything strange on the golf course?'

'Two leverets. Playward, they were. Like as if a great joy were in them.'

'Ah, yes.' Appleby was familiar with Solo's propensity to sidestep awkward issues by way of poetical reflection. Here was a striking instance of it. Which meant that there *was* something awkward. There was something, that was to say, which Solo judged it would be hazardous to admit cognizance of. So Appleby decided to take a chance, and move in. 'Solo,' he said, 'you saw something. And Jem too, I expect. It was at the bunker. The bunker where the body was found. Or *wasn't* found. You saw somebody, didn't you?'

Solo said nothing. But he very slowly shook his head.

'I don't want to have the police from Linger coming and asking you questions. Or asking Jem. So tell me, please. For instance, did you see Bobby?'

'We ne'er had sight o' Mr Bobby.' Solo had spoken surprisingly quickly.

'Nobody is suspecting Bobby of anything. He has nothing to hide.' Appleby wondered whether these were ideas within or without Solo's conceptual range. 'Just what did you see?'

Appleby paused hopefully. But Solo had changed gear again. He simply shook his head even more slowly than before.

'Mr Robert,' Appleby said with some formality, 'simply must know what you and Jem saw. It is most important to him. So speak up.'

'He hasn't axed me, Mr Bobby hasn't.' Solo looked almost cunning. He was determined not to be tricked.

'That's because he isn't here, Solo. He went away without knowing that you and Jem had been near the golf-course. But he'd want you to tell me. Out with it, Solo, and then you can get on with your work.'

'Urr.' It was impossible to tell what attitude to honest toil Solo's favourite vocable (learnt from his elderly relative) was intended to convey. But now he took a deep breath, and Appleby realised that something was coming at last. 'There were a rake,' Solo said.

'A rake?' For a moment Appleby was at a loss. 'Where were you when you saw a rake?'

'Coming out of thicket where we slep. But we stopped-like, unbeknownst.'

'Nobody saw either of you?'

'Had rabbits.'

'Yes, of course. You thought you might be spotted with your rabbits, so you stayed in hiding. What was the first thing you saw?'

'Car on road.'

'There was a car with a trailer. I can see you are telling the truth, Solo. Bobby would be very pleased with you. And what was the next thing that you saw after that?'

'Men running.'

'How many men?'

'The two men carrying it might be a bed.'

'Carrying a bed? Do you mean a stretcher?'

Solo looked blank. His vocabulary was not extensive.

'These two men were running with their bed or stretcher towards the bunker? And there was a body in the bunker?'

'Certain there were body in bunker.' Solo seemed indisposed to accord any special emphasis to the circumstance. 'And there were this rake.'

'In the bunker too?'

'Only ball were in bunker. Ball and corpus.'

'I know there was a ball. But where was the rake?'

'Rake were wi' wench. Wench were running wi' rake, and men were running wi' bed. Wench had picked up rake, might be, from shelter by second tee.'

'It was very quick-witted of her.' Appleby's voice had changed. 'Listen, Solo. I am going to tell you what happened then. These three people ran to the bunker. The men put the body on the stretcher, and hurried back to the car with it. The wench—she was a young girl—stayed to rake over the bunker, and then she ran back after them. They put the body in the trailer, and drove away at once. Is that right?'

'That be right.' Solo was reproachful. 'You never said you a-been there too.'

'No more I was. Why haven't you told anybody about this?'

''Twere no affair of ours, Jem nor me. Had rabbits.' A large rationality now seemed to attend Solo's utterance. 'And foreigners, they been. Nought had it to do wi' folk from Dream nor Stony Dream nor Boxer's Bottom. Not even from Linger itself or the Yatters, they were. Happen they came from distant parts. Long Snarl, it might be. Or from other kingdoms. Little Sneak, belike, or Abbot's Amble.'

128

'No doubt. Now listen, Solo. This is very important. You say you saw nothing of Mr Robert? You didn't, immediately after this, see him coming from the club-house to the bunker?'

'No sight of Mr Bobby.'

'Nor of a little group of men, one of whom might have been Mr Robert?'

'All we seen you now know.' Solo produced this surprisingly succinct statement almost crisply. 'We bain't nesh, Jem nor me. But we bain't fools neither. Had rabbits. Ran.'

CHAPTER EIGHT

So MUCH—APPLEBY told himself as he walked slowly back to the house—for the young woman in whose service Bobby had chosen to set off as a knight errant. Perhaps she had actually murdered the man upon whom Bobby had come in the bunker. If she had not, she had certainly been an accessory after the fact. She had distracted Bobby in the moment that there was a danger of his identifying the corpse. She had got him off to the telephone and had herself made hard for the car—the occupants of which were in fact her accomplices. She had hurried them back to the bunker—it had almost certainly been *back*—bearing the stretcher upon which the body had presumably been conveyed to it in the first place. The body had then been removed to the car or its trailer, and the girl had been quick-witted enough to find and do her job with that rake. And of *that* the consequence had been that Bobby could be aspersed as imagining things.

And so indeed he could. Appleby came momentarily to a halt as the force of this was born in upon him. Girl, confederates, corpse and all had disappeared into the blue. And so had Bobby—his head full of the rash assumption that he was in quest of an abducted heroine.

Neither living nor dead had Nauze—Bloody Nauze— ever been within Appleby's view. But now, suddenly in his own garden, Appleby seemed to see Nauze very clearly indeed—as a dead body with a good part of its head shot off. And this, one might say, was the measure of the savagery of the affair in which Bobby—under a vast illusion which made him hideously vulnerable—had gone hurtling off to involve himself. Not, of course, that there was any crisis. Even on the assumption that the dead man was indeed Nauze, all that Bobby was at present engaged upon was trying to pick up at Overcombe what would almost certainly be a very cold trail upon that long-departed Latin master. It was true that it mightn't be healthy for Bobby if the obviously ruthless people involved in the crime got to know that a young man was chasing them up even at that remove. But there was not the slightest reason to suppose that Overcombe was any longer in the picture at all. The probability was that Bobby would return unscathed but baffled from what had proved to be a wild-goose chase. The important thing, meanwhile, was to make rather more sense of the mystery than either Appleby himself or anybody else had yet been able to do.

The telephone call. The spurious telephone call which had represented itself as coming from the Home Office, and by which Sergeant Howard had not unnaturally been taken in. As Appleby found his mind going back to this, he reflected that Howard had at least come to an acute conclusion about it. Bobby's adventure had got in rather an imprecise way into an early edition of an evening paper —and almost at once some unknown person had attempted to check up on it. The affair of the bunker was far from being a one-man show, Howard had said. And there were villains who weren't trusting one another very far.

It was a good inference—and, if only uncertainly, one could get a little further on the basis of it. Indeed, Appleby had already done so. The body had been put where it *had* been put with a definite purpose in view—and that purpose looked like being the ensuring of its discovery within a certain limit of time. But there had been a hitch—and that hitch was Bobby. The body was to be *found*; it was *not* to be identified. Because of the danger of that, it had been snatched away again. *And this had left somebody— presumably not one of the snatchers—in doubt about some vital point.* Had Nauze (to call him that) been killed at all? If he had, had he been safely dead by the time some-body was claiming he had been safely dead? But what could be the context of such a situation? Appleby had made a shot or two at guessing. But he didn't feel that, so far, he had come upon a hypothesis that satisfied him.

Could anything be arrived at by simply considering the *dramatis personae*? The trouble was that any persons who could be so described were uncommonly thin on the ground. It was no good perpending the character and situation of Robert Appleby. That Robert Appleby had a hinterland (scrum-half Appleby, author-of-*The-Lumber-Room* Appleby) was neither here nor there, since the entry of Robert Appleby into the affair had plainly been purely fortuitous. That left Nauze (*if* Nauze) and the girl. Nauze lacked a finger. Nauze had once possessed a gym-shoe. Nauze had been an usher in a superior academy for young gentlemen. Nauze had taught Latin notably well. End of information on background of Nauze. The girl had been capable of powerfully attracting Robert Appleby (afore-said). End of information on the girl.

Or not quite. The girl who had powerfully attracted Bobby had been mixed up in funny business with the corpse of a murdered man.

Sir John Appleby, remaining stock-still on the garden side of Long Dream Manor, stared very hard (if meta-phorically) at this solid fact (for it was a solid fact) of the situation. He then broke into notably rapid motion, gained thereby the modest but eastward-facing apartment in which he had breakfasted, and stared very hard (but non-figuratively, this time) at the newspapers he had lately abandoned there. Not a word. *Not a word.* For the first time, there glimmered on the verges of the affair of the bunker a faint penumbra of sense. People foxing each other. And a girl—*that* sort of girl capable of seducing Bobby Appleby even when she didn't at all mean to—

running around disposing of corpses. Yes! Just conceivably, it added up.

Mrs Colpoys was in the breakfast-room.

'Sergeant Howard, sir,' she said.

And Howard was shown in. He entered with an air entirely proper in a warrant-officer (as it might be) seeking
an interview with (say) a retired Adjutant-General or Chief
of the Imperial General Staff. But this did not for a
moment disguise the fact that Howard was a very angry
man.

'Sir,' Howard said, 'I have no business here. None at all.'

'Then I wish it were an hour at which I could offer you a
drink. Come to think of it, I can. Mrs Colpoys will still
have coffee going. I'll just chase after her.' Appleby went
to the door. 'No bells left in this house,' he explained
amiably. 'All torn out by the roots by some Raven or other
in a rage. You're a local man, Sergeant?'

'Man and boy, Sir John.'

'Then you know about my wife's people. I shan't be a
moment. Cigarettes in that box. Or light your pipe. I've
plenty of time for a talk. You'll find that yourself, when
you retire.'

These composing remarks had a certain effect. When
Appleby returned—with Mrs Colpoys hard behind him—
Howard had distinguishably calmed down.

'You mustn't blame the Colonel,' Appleby said.

'Sir?' There was proper surprise in Howard's tone.

'Come, Sergeant. Haven't you been told to lay off, more
or less?'

'Something like that, Sir John. And I don't like it. It's
not fair on your son. A nice lad, if I may say so. That's
why I've called. I dare say I might be hauled over the coals
for it.'

'I dare say you might. Your Chief Constable's a very

good man. Army background, of course, and all that.'

'Yes, Sir.'

'Accepts orders, Sergeant, and expects to have his own accepted.'

'Orders, sir?' Sergeant Howard frowned. 'I take his. But where should his come from? Not from London, unless I have a very wrong notion of the legal position of the Constabulary.'

'You haven't. Clearly you haven't. But sometimes, I suppose, there are overruling considerations.'

'No doubt, sir.' Howard's tone didn't suggest that he was prepared to allow much to this. 'There's no damned body. That's the mischief.'

'It would be simpler if there was a body?'

'Of course it would. The Coroner would have to sit on it. But there's no body. There's nothing but a story told by your son. A true story.'

'You judge it to be a true story?'

'I thought I'd made that clear to you already, Sir John.' Howard spoke stiffly. 'I consider Mr Appleby's testimony to be wholly reliable.'

'So does Colonel Pride, doesn't he?'

'Well, yes. I think he does. But he takes these orders—'

'Which are not orders, at all?'

'Of course they're not. The Prime Minister himself couldn't give such an order. I doubt whether the Queen in Council could.'

'I see you are a student of the Constitution, Sergeant. I was interested in it myself. But, of course, there are other powers.' Appleby pointed to the newspapers on a table. 'Not a word.'

'Just so, sir.'

'At least it tells us something. You and I.'

'That's very true sir.' Howard had brightened. 'It does give us a line.'

'Ought we to have a line? Is it at all our affair?'

'It's your son's affair, Sir John.'

'So it is.' For a moment Appleby was silent. 'It's also *their* affair. Do you want me to say whether I have any confidence in them?'

'It wouldn't be a proper question for me to ask.'

'No more it would. But—implicitly, at least—you *are* asking it. Well, it's my impression that they're better than they were.'

'That may well be.'

'Yes. But they keep some of their old vices—or is it virtues?—still. Mum's the word.'

'Sir?'

'A mania for covering up. And—as my man Hoobin says—always the right hand not knowing what the left hand doth. It's not the technique you and I were brought up in, Sergeant.'

'Decidedly not. And I'm wondering whether there's anything you can do, sir. You see what the position is. But for that newspaper report—which is the kind of thing nobody remembers after three or four days—there's nothing. Nothing public, I mean. And there's nothing *at all* except your son's report to us.'

'And your telephone call that was supposed to come from the Home Office.'

'Well, yes—but that might just be a joker who had read the paragraph in the paper. So the evidence is simply Mr Appleby's statement. Now, suppose nothing more ever happens. Anybody who remembers anything at all about the matter will vaguely suppose that some sort of hoax was being played upon the police. There would be nothing which could be called particularly injurious to Mr Appleby's reputation in that. So one can see that the Chief Constable is rather awkwardly placed when he gets this hint or order or whatever to let be. As I say, it's the lack of the body that cripples us. If we just had *that*, we could force these people's hand if we wanted to.'

'We could do nothing without consultation with them, Sergeant. Ten to one, what we are witnessing is simply their conventional hugger-mugger and instinct to cover up. But it's just possibly something quite different. They may want no further action, no further publicity, for some very weighty reason indeed.'

'Well, I can see that. But a totally illegal embargo on a normal police investigation doesn't please me. Particularly when its effect is to brand a respectable young man like Mr Appleby as either deluded or frivolous.'

'My dear Howard, I very much appreciate your feeling that way.' Appleby paused, and glared through the high mullioned window of the breakfast-room. Solo Hoobin had finished clearing the lawn of its litter, and was now preparing to ride up and down it on the mowing-machine. It was having been given the freedom of this exciting implement within the secure boundaries of Dream that had first put into Solo's head the more hazardous ambition of owning a moped. Solo swung the engine as Appleby watched, and then stood back with a kind of proprietary pride at the resulting roar. The ancient Hoobin had now appeared, and had plainly appointed as his morning's task the onerous business of directing his nephew's further progress. Appleby got up and closed the window. 'So there is something I must tell you,' he said.

'Sir?'

'What you would like to have—say, what you and the Chief Constable would both like to have—is a little independent evidence. Evidence, I mean, that there *was* a body —that there was a body and a girl and a motor-car with a trailer-caravan and a couple of strange men. The whole set-up that we know perfectly well Bobby did *not* imagine. I think that's right?'

'It wouldn't come amiss, Sir John. Of course, we wouldn't act irresponsibly. But it would be satisfactory, shall we say, to have something of the kind under our hand.'

'As a matter of fact, we have.' Appleby pointed through the window. 'Do you know that lad of mine out there—Solo Hoobin?'

'Yes, I do—although nothing against him.' Howard sounded doubtful. 'A bit of a natural, isn't he?'

'Well, Sergeant, that's our old-fashioned word for it. They'd now call Solo E.S.N. Educationally subnormal. I dare say he was never much of a candidate for the Eleven Plus. Still, he has eyes in his head.'

'You mean, sir, that this young man saw—?'

'The body in the bunker. And then the two men and the girl making off with it. It was on a poaching expedition on Monday night and Tuesday morning.'

'Good heavens!' As he uttered this exclamation, Sergeant Howard sprang to his feet. 'If I'd known—'

'It came to me only half-an-hour ago, Sergeant. It was pure chance that I started getting it out of Solo at all. He didn't want trouble.'

'They never do.' Howard frowned. 'He wouldn't—would he?—make much of a witness, sir.'

'He had a companion of his own age called Jem Puckrup, whom I haven't seen. Quite a different type is Jem. As sharp as they come. No magistrate could take it into his head that Jem had been dreaming something up.' Appleby paused. 'Will you have another cup of coffee?' he asked.

Howard had sat down again, but not without evident reluctance. He had been given a lead, and it was his impulse to follow it up at once. Solo Hoobin, in fact, had come very near to being whisked off to the police station at Linger—an event which would have alarmed him very much. Given his head, Howard would have had Jem Puckrup in too—and Jem would in consequence be in a position to enjoy several glorious evenings of free beer at the Killcanon Arms on the strength of his experience. Appleby judged this undesirable. It would, of course, be entirely impossible for him to withhold from either Howard or Colonel Pride the information he had come by from Solo. But, as an interim measure at least, he wanted his own way with it now.

'Would you think of having a word with those two lads, Sergeant?' he asked diplomatically.

'Well, yes. It would only be in order, sir, if I may say so.'

'Perfectly right. Would you care to ring through to the Chief Constable now? You'll find the telephone in the library entirely private.'

'You think I ought to have his authority, Sir John?' It was unmistakable that Howard wasn't too pleased.

'Well, I do think that you and I, Sergeant, must both mind our step. This is a delicate matter, whether we like it or not. And perhaps we should consider where we stand with these two lads now. The major likelihood is that we already know everything material that they have to tell. But I don't put it higher than that, mark you. You might well pick up from Solo out there something that I let slip by me.'

'I don't think that's at all probable, sir.' Howard was already mollified.

'But there's another side to the thing. As the matter stands, both Solo and Jem will continue to keep quiet. Solo thinks of me as reliable. He probably won't let on to Jem Puckrup that he's told his story. And their chief thought, as I said, is to keep out of trouble. Once the police tackle them, and they know they're involved, their motive for keeping their mouths shut will be gone. They'll have a high old time spinning their yarn.'

'Quite true, sir. But where there's been violence and possibly murder, one doesn't like to have uninterrogated witnesses at risk.'

'They're not at risk—unless in point of mere accident. They took care to keep well out of sight on Tuesday morning, and you and I are at present the only people in the world who know their story. Nobody can possibly be after them.'

'Yes, Sir John. But that doesn't apply to your son.'

Howard had at least reduced Appleby to a moment's silence. When he did speak, it was soberly enough.

'You think Bobby may be running into mischief?'

'Well, sir, I don't imagine he's simply taken himself off on a holiday. And this doesn't look like being an affair for amateurs.'

'Bobby is certainly that. And it looks as if he may have a dangerously erroneous notion of this girl. But I don't think he can have got anywhere very far as yet. His only line, you see, has been the possibility that the dead man was a master at his first school—a place called Overcombe. That's where Bobby has gone off to, I believe. It's rather a wide cast, if you ask me. And does give us a little time.'

'I don't agree.' Howard had stood up again—and Appleby saw that he was the same angry man who had presented himself half-an-hour before. 'This is no sort of affair to mark time on, if you ask me. And it's something that, in your position, you don't need to do. The Chief Constable is an important man, no doubt. He has to be listened to, and given a civil reply. But not more than that. He doesn't *know* people, Sir John, any more than I do. But can't you get what information you want? You must have top connections far outside the Metropolitan Police. Wouldn't it be a good idea—just for your own satisfaction, and without relaying anything to me—to get into the picture, and know just what's going on?'

'If anything *is* going on—in the sense we have in mind. It's still not quite certain, Howard, that the whole affair isn't a perfectly ordinary sort of crime.'

'It would be very satisfactory to know that, sir. Very satisfactory, indeed.'

'I take your point, Sergeant.' Appleby was silent for a

moment, and then got to his feet. 'I'll see what I can do.'

And at that, as was only proper, Sergeant Howard took his departure at once. He paused on his way down the drive—Appleby noted with amusement—to give Solo Hoobin a casual greeting and an appraising glance. Left to himself, Appleby experienced two or three minutes of something like irresolution. And then, very unusually, he spoke to himself aloud.

'The fellow's quite right,' he said. He went into the library, picked up the telephone, and glanced at the clock. Half-past-ten. The morning was still young.

Part Four

THE GIRL

CHAPTER NINE

SLIPPING OUT OF the Leather Bottle, Bobby Appleby looked at his watch. Ten to seven. Prep would be almost over, and in the next quarter of an hour he must make his rendezvous with Beadon and Walcot. But here, meanwhile, was the girl—miraculously proposing, it seemed, to eat out of his hand. He glanced back through the door before closing it. Jakin and Lew were finishing their brandies at leisure; they had rather lost interest in their casual entertainer as soon as he had paid for this quite costly form of refreshment. But they would be following him out in a minute or two. He signed rapidly to the girl, and dodged round to the back of the pub.

She followed him, and they were face to face.

'Off duty?' he asked.

'In one sense, yes. We're talking. Where's your car?'

'Still in the school drive. Walk down to the lodge and I'll overtake you. We're dining.'

'Perhaps.'

'No perhaps about it, Susan Danbury. You've got a lot of awkward lies to explain. The Three Feathers is quite good, and only four miles away. I'm putting up there.'

'Not proper to dine with a gentleman where he's putting up.'

'Stop talking nonsense, and listen. I've got to see two of the boys first. Beadon and Walcot. I've taken them on as my assistants. Like the boy Tinker in Sexton Blake. And I've a date with them in ten minutes' time. Your turn after that.'

'Thank you very much. But, just for the moment, please

follow me. Our association is to be quite an innocent one, Bobby Appleby. But we're not advertising it, all the same.' As she said this, Susan walked rapidly off. It didn't occur to Bobby *not* to follow. His heart was pounding just as if the whistle was about to blow at the end of a gruelling first half. He doubted whether he was going to be good at a game of wits with Susan—if it was adversaries, that was to say, they were going to be. There were nice girls with whom he'd tumbled around a bit. But none of his Away Matches had been anything like this at all.

Susan had vanished—and then he realised that she had simply slipped into a disused stable. She seemed to know the surroundings of the Leather Bottle pretty well.

'What have you told them?' she asked, as he followed her in.

'Beadon and Walcot? I've told them I belong in a spy-story.' Bobby heard Susan catch her breath. 'Odd, don't you think? It just came into my head as a means of interesting them. I don't even know if they believed me. And the funny thing is, it's true.'

'Where are you going to meet them?'

'A sunken place just off the drive. I found them smoking there.'

'Well, go and meet them. And promise me something.'

'Anything in the world. *Anything*. You see, Susan, I'm going to marry you as soon as they let you out of gaol. The ceremony will be performed by the prison chaplain, with the Archbishop of Canterbury lending a hand. He's my godfather, you see.'

'Will you please be serious?' For a moment, it was almost as if Miss Danbury was a little at a loss. 'You must promise to dismiss these boys. Tell them it was all nonsense, and that they're to put it out of their heads.'

'I expect you're right.' This time, Bobby *was* serious. 'The spy-story isn't developing like kids' stuff.'

'It didn't begin that way either, so far as you were concerned. You saw what you saw—you saw what *we* saw—in the bunker.'

'Yes,' Bobby said, and looked Susan very straight in the eye. At last she seemed to be coming clean. 'That was far from being kids' stuff, I agree. And I oughtn't to have pitched Beadon and Walcot a yarn. But, you see, it's something that sometimes happens with me, quite suddenly. It's because I write things, I suppose. Did I tell you I'm a writer? It's something you'll have to put up with, I'm afraid. All sorts of other things too, I suppose. But I'll have one virtue. I'm going to be faithful to you. Until I die.'

'Which may be quite soon.' Susan Danbury got this out so crisply that it almost covered up the way her lips had parted a fraction of a second before. 'But not those children, please.'

'All right.'

'Bobby, I'm *deadly* serious. There's a grim battle on, and we've begun with a shattering defeat. I'm not going to have two small boys—'

'I promise. And I'll go now. But—Susan—one thing. You said *we've* begun with—'

'Are you an idiot?' It seemed to Bobby that Susan was really staring at him round-eyed. 'Am I a beautiful Russian? Are you making all those amorous remarks—'

'Not amorous remarks. It's what they call being in love. At least I suppose it is.'

'Whatever it is, do you think you're really offering it to a bloody Mata Hari? Don't you credit yourself with any sense?' Miss Danbury paused in this brilliant counter-offensive—but not long enough to permit Bobby to do more than begin mumbling something. 'You find your kids,' she said, 'and I'll find your car. I'll like our dinner, honest Bobby Appleby. But don't expect it to be a lingering one.' Again she paused for only a moment. 'You leave this shed first, please. If anybody's around, they'll think you've been answering what's termed a natural call. And give a whistle when all's clear.'

Half an hour later, they drove in complete silence to the Three Feathers. The trip took over six minutes, so this was perhaps a little odd. They had a drink at the bar, and failed to get beyond discussing the menu perched on it. Bobby was far from regarding this topic as trivial—for weren't they going to recall this meal, Susan and he, in minute detail forty years on? The Three Feathers was said to be reliable—but ought they to begin by playing safe, and simply have smoked salmon for a start? Nothing much could go wrong with *that*. But Susan voted this down, and they ordered, in a spirit of experiment, an obscure concoction described as a speciality of the house. Bobby was enchanted by this intimation of divergent temperaments. It would be much more fun, he told himself, that way.

'We can't go on being civilised,' Susan said suddenly, when they had sat down at table. 'Defer talking turkey, I mean, until after the soufflé. How did you manage with Beadon and Walcot?'

'I did my best. It wasn't awfully easy. You see, they've been noticing things. I forgot to tell you that.'

'What sort of thing?'

'Oh, Nauze himself—although they don't know his name. And a nocturnal helicopter.'

'I see.' Susan didn't seem terribly impressed. 'Anything else?'

'Two bearded Russians.'

'Nonsense!' This time, Susan spoke sharply. 'Such people aren't *seen*. The boys were having you on.'

'So I might have supposed. But, as it happens, I've seen them myself. This afternoon, as I was coming down from a walk near the Great Smithy.'

'Did you tell Beadon and Walcot that?'

'Yes, I thought it best to. I explained that these two

chaps were certainly foreigners, but that they were perfectly ordinary walkers, all the same.' Bobby paused. 'Susan, why have you changed your mind about me?'

'I haven't. I've merely had orders to change it.' She looked at him with perfect gravity. 'I've never been other than of one mind about you.'

'I'd like to know what that is.' Bobby's heart had bounded. 'If I may,' he added humbly.

'It's not what's really relevant now.' Susan dug her fork into the conglomeration of chilled sea-foods before her. 'I was right about this. It's fab.' She took a quick glance round the dining-room of the Three Feathers, and then continued without a pause. 'I hope I *shan't* go to gaol. It did no good to Nauze.'

'He'd been in gaol?' Bobby stared at Susan in astonishment. 'Was that why he left Overcombe rather abruptly donkeys' years ago?'

'No, it wasn't. You know nothing whatever about all this —do you, Bobby?'

'Why should I? Didn't I just blunder into it? But I've been picking things up.' Bobby smiled cheerfully. 'I've picked you up, for example.' He paused while the waiter uncorked a bottle of wine. 'Susan, how did you come by your extraordinary profession—or what I take to be your profession?'

'That's not quite relevant either. But the answer's quite simple.' She broke off. 'Do you know that we were undergraduates together?'

'It's impossible. I couldn't have missed you. Not among a mere thousand girls. Not even amoung a hundred thousand citizens.'

'I didn't miss *you*. I used to be taken to see Rugger matches and things.'

'Did you like them?'

'Not terribly. Rugger struck me as rather a brutal sort of game.'

'I see.' Bobby thought fleetingly of Nauze, sprawled in the bunker with half his head blown off. 'I've given it up,' he said reassuringly.

'Yes—I suppose you must be getting on.'

'I'm not getting on.' Bobby was indignant. 'It's just that I've taken up some other things.'

'Intellectual pursuits. And now a spot of—well, this. Which, as I say, you know nothing whatever about. Just why did you come plunging over here?'

'I thought it might give me a line on Nauze. And that that might give me a line on you. You'd vanished, and I was determined to find you. It looked as if you might be in a bit of a fix, you know, and that I might lend a hand. But you still haven't told me how you came to take up this sort of thing.'

'Influence. Wire-pulling.' Susan gazed at Bobby with a great appearance of ingenuousness. 'I didn't terribly like a women's college at Oxford. For one thing, there were too many young men.'

'I'm sure there were.'

'But I had this uncle—'

'M.,' Bobby suggested. 'I take my orders from him, as a matter of fact. I'm 008.'

'You're a perfect menace, it seems to me. But I had this uncle, as I say, and one thing has led to another.'

'Your uncle behaved most irresponsibily in signing on his own niece for such a career.'

'Such an unwomanly career. I suppose so. Probably he wouldn't, as a matter of fact, if he'd known it would take me into—well, rather active work. But shall we get back to Nauze, Bobby? You'd better know at least the one salient fact about him.'

'I think I better had.' Bobby found that when Susan *called* him Bobby his head swam. 'What is it—or was it?'

'Nauze was the most brilliant cryptographer on the face of this earth. More brilliant than Rashidov, even.'

'Who would be the Russians' top man on ciphers?'

'Yes.'

'That shattering defeat you spoke of—it was Nauze's death?'

There was a pause, while Susan Danbury took her first sip of wine.

'Yes,' she said. 'Just that.'

The dining-room of the Three Feathers was filling up. This was to be expected. The pub had its entry in the various guides to good eating and the like, and it was even an entry that seemed pretty well deserved. They wouldn't look back with affection on that absolutely awful first meal together; they would look back on that modestly excellent one. But they had a table in a deep window-embrasure, and it wasn't possible that they could be overheard.

'He was caught seven years ago,' Susan said quietly. 'It sounds rather a stupid business; he had just gone on holiday somewhere he had no business to. And he was recognised. Perhaps that finger. Of course, he was a bit of a drunk, which didn't help. Not all that. And it had already been a complication.'

'He took a gym-shoe to us when he was a bit tight.'

'It wouldn't have done *you* much harm.' Susan was quite unimpressed. 'But I know about that. It's all in his file.'

'You don't mean to say that Nauze was doing his stuff —cracking codes, or whatever—back when he was a master at Overcombe?'

'Certainly he was—and absolutely at the top of his form then. What has happened lately a bit turned on that. He had a very odd mind, it seems. A kind of *Finnegans Wake* mind as far as command of language went, but also a highly mathematical mind as well. It was the combination that put him at the head of his profession.'

'It certainly doesn't seem too bright to have allowed him to be captured by someone. But one's not a spy, surely, if one simply sits in an office and cracks codes?'

'He'd had other assignments, and there was plenty of evidence against him. So it was a fair cop, in a way.'

'Did he manage to escape?'

'Oh, no. It was just one of those quiet exchanges. And he was back in London before we realised—I mean, before my bosses realised—that we looked like being badly sold. Nauze was what's called a broken man.'

'Good God! Had they been torturing him?'

'I don't suppose so. No, I'm sure they hadn't. Top-flight people like Nauze are always potentially too valuable to be treated to that.' Susan paused. This particular aspect of things seemed not to trouble her. 'I don't suppose they so much as took a gym-shoe to him. But something went badly wrong. Perhaps it began with malnutrition or something. Do you remember Michaelis in *The Secret Agent*?'

'Not very well.' Bobby was enchanted that Susan read books. He wondered whether she'd read *The Lumber Room*, anti-novel by R. Appleby.

'I do. I've a good memory. It's the principal thing that enables me to hold down my job, as a matter of fact. Michaelis had been inside. He had come out of a highly hygienic prison round like a tub, with an enormous stomach and distended cheeks of a pale, semi-transparent complexion, as though for fifteen years the servants of an outraged society had made a point of stuffing him with fattening foods in a damp and lightless cellar.' Susan finished her first glass of wine. 'That's more or less *verbatim*, I believe.'

'And quite irrelevant. You're showing off.' Bobby got in this thrust with high delight. 'For I don't believe Nauze came back like that.'

'He didn't. He came back with what appeared a shattering nervous breakdown. The trick-cyclists got going on him. They said No, it wasn't that, but a straight galloping psychosis. Then they had another look, and said it was a nervous breakdown after all. And some genius thought up Overcombe. Which is what was to bring me there. Bobby, I didn't know such places *were*.'

'You talk awfully well, Susan.'

'I'll talk. You'll write.'

Bobby's head swam even worse than it had ever done before. Susan had this queer trade. It required what was hard-boiled in her manner. But, having made up her mind, she was as direct as Perdita. *No, like a bank for love to lie and play on.* A sudden overwhelming impatience seized Bobby—not (as would have been proper in 008) to possess her forthwith, for that might be aeons off, and was certainly not now to be imagined. Bobby was simply impatient to bring this sinister and fantastic business to an end, and to stand in Susan's presence in a context fit for so standing.

'This has to be over by midnight,' he heard himself say. And he heard himself add—as if with some concession to humour—'Or by breakfast-time, anyway.'

'You think it might be?' Her tone was cool and even mocking. But, just before she had spoken, her lips had parted again. 'That would be very nice, of course.'

'You'll never again have anything that isn't nice.' Bobby stared at her—the dream girl, who must have nothing but truth. 'Except from crass casualty and blind fate. And now, give me the rest of the gen about this wretched luckless Nauze. Straight through, please. No more bits and pieces.'

'Very well. But, please, may I have another glass of wine? And half-a-glass later on? That means three and a half, all-told, for you.'

'Mostly,' Bobby said, 'it will be a half-bottle between us. And beer on Thursdays. But go ahead.'

'Then, here goes.' Susan glanced round the dining-room again, and then looked at her watch ... 'It's not altogether polite,' she said, 'to be worried about the time, when having one's first dinner with an eligible young man. But, you see, time has been of the essence in this whole business. Now listen.'

CHAPTER TEN

'SOME GENIUS THOUGHT of Overcombe. I'd got as far as that. You see the idea. Nauze was to be got back into the environment in which he had enjoyed his first triumphs in a code-cracking way. Confidence would return to him amid the happy voices of the boys.'

'Alas, regardless of their doom, the little victims play.'

'Don't interrupt. When he was got some way into his right mind he might even do a little teaching, which would be another step in reconstituting the old Nauze. And they seem to have thought, too, that Overcombe would be a marvellously unobtrusive place in which to quarter him. That, of course, was a quite shocking miscalculation. It was true that in his first period as a master in the school his activities as a cryptographer had remained utterly secret. But it was equally true that he might well have mentioned it under interrogation when inside. It wouldn't seem important, and when in prison people of that sort are always being offered small privileges in return for even scraps of information. Anyway, the fact is that we have probably been under observation from the very start of the set-up.'

'Gulliver and Onslow must have been in on this?'

'Certainly. I don't know that they were very keen, and I expect they were distinctly evasive when you started sniffing after news of Nauze this morning.'

'Yes. And Onslow was furious that Gulliver invited me to lunch.'

'I expect that was just jealousy of a *bona-fide* athlete, Bobby dear. But they've both been quite good, really. Then, of course, there has been Hartsilver. He was the only other person around the place at all likely to remember or recognize Nauze. A great deal was to depend on Hartsilver.'

'He was quite shockingly disingenuous with me when I went to see him. He seemed thoroughly communicative, but in fact kept entirely mum. I just wouldn't have believed it of him.'

'Hartsilver has missed his *métier*.'

'I know. He has some sort of disease that makes it impossible for him to paint.'

'I don't mean that. Hartsilver would have been superb at Intelligence stuff. Absolutely a master spy. *And* tiptop at codes and so forth as well.'

'Oh, come! I can't—'

'It's perfectly true—and the fact contains the germ of any real justification for bringing Nauze back to Overcombe. These two had been very thick indeed. Hartsilver was considerably older, of course. But, in the technique of the thing, he was very much Nauze's pupil. A posthumous pupil at this moment, one might say.'

'Whatever do you mean by that?'

'Hartsilver's trying to do what Nauze might have done.'

At this point Susan was constrained to pause in her exploitation of the distinctly peculiar state of affairs at Overcombe School. This was because she and Bobby had earlier decided on concluding their meal with one of those confections which involve a lavish cracking of eggs, kindling of chafing-dishes, and flourishing of liqueur-bottles in the immediate vicinity of the gratified diners. The impressive ritual was being performed now. It required the joint efforts of the head waiter of the Three Feathers and of a man dressed like a *chef* who had emerged from the kitchens for the purpose. Bobby, since it was he who had conjured the operation into being, felt obliged to watch it with an experienced and critical eye. The big moment was when the whole thing caught on fire. It was the bigger because one was never able to tell whether or not it was an unrehearsed effect. The chaps always seemed to have it under control—but not all that under control. The satisfaction which slightly younger people get from the entry of a Christmas-pudding sheathed in a flicker of blue flame, or of a birthday-cake with candles, was what Mr Robert Appleby (*jeune écrivain anglais d'une distinction indubitable*, as he had been courteously described) and his affianced bride (as she may now virtually be called) had been proposing to themselves now. In fact, they were rather anxious that these two superior members of the staff of the Three Feathers should get through their stuff and go away.

Bobby watched carefully, nevertheless. And the conflagration, when it came, was quite notable of its kind. A very large and brilliant sheet of flame leapt up from the pan in which the *soufflé* omelette was being prepared. And in the middle of it—to a wholly Mephistophelean effect—Bobby was suddenly aware of a bearded face.

The flame flared and faded. The face vanished. Bobby found that he was staring fixedly at the door of the dining-room.

'Did you see that?' Bobby asked.

'Of course. The thrill's because it's mildly criminal, don't you think? Burning up perfectly good alk.'

'I don't mean that. I mean one of your Russian friends, or whatever they are. He made a brief inspection of us from the doorway.'

'Then it's quite smart of him to be chasing us up.' Susan was unperturbed. 'But I can't think why they keep on hanging around. They brought off their assignment, after all.'

'Which was?'

'Killing Nauze, of course.' Susan seemed surprised that there could be any uncertainty about this. 'I suppose they want to pick up better proof of their achievement. For is

Nauze *really* dead? Not many people know—apart from you and me. We foxed them there a bit.'

There had to be another pause, since the omelette—adequately *flambée*—was now being served. Bobby employed it by trying to pull his thoughts together. He kept on—it seemed to him—beginning to get on top of this bizarre affair, only to find it taking another turn that surpassed ready belief.

'If they killed Nauze,' he asked rather weakly, 'don't you think they ought to be arrested?'

'We're not in quite that sort of world at the moment.' Susan frowned. 'But they *oughtn't* to be around. They can't possibly know about Hartsilver. Aren't you going to finish the wine?'

'No, and neither are you. I don't like being spied on by your bearded friend—particularly when he seems to have you guessing a bit. I think we need clear heads. And now let's have the rest of your story.'

'Very well. And order some coffee.' Susan pushed away her glass. 'The slightly strange part is still to come.' She paused as if expecting to be challenged on this, but Bobby said nothing. 'I mean the time-element chiefly. There's been a date-line, you see, for getting Nauze on his feet again. Or getting him into play again. A zero-hour. And so the other side has had a zero-hour too. From their point of view, there was a day and an hour by which Nauze—if at all recovered, and they were taking no risks—had to be dead. Of course we didn't know this. We didn't know they'd spotted our Overcombe set-up at all.' Susan paused to light a cigarette. 'Do you know about anti-ballistic missiles?'

'Yes. They're cock-eyed.'

'No doubt. Well in some remote place or other, something bang-new had been picked up about them—'

'Bang sounds the right word.'

'Be quiet. A development of staggering importance,

achieved by a not too friendly power. But the information about this bang-new thing was concealed in a bang-new code. The document was being flown to London. And then it would come to Overcombe—'

'By helicopter?'

'Certainly by helicopter. For Nauze to have a go at. It looked like Nauze or nobody.'

'Those not-too-friendly-power chaps sound even more half-witted than our own.'

'Don't be so damned superior.'

'Sorry—but you see what I mean. Exchanging this Nauze character for anybody at all.'

'They judged he was finished, as I've said. And they were possibly right or possibly wrong. But they *did* decide they'd made a bloomer. Hence Nauze's death being decided upon as soon as they got wind of the Overcombe plan—the plan to rehabilitate the poor devil. The job was assigned to a couple of quite inconsiderable and low-class killers. You've met them.'

'Were they the two men with the car and the caravan on the edge of the golf-course?'

'Bobby, for pity's sake! I've told you already it was your bearded friends.'

'But mayn't *they* have been on the golf-course?'

'As a matter of fact, *they were*. But not the way you think. Now go on listening. You must conceive these bearded men as simply having accepted a commission to liquidate Nauze within a certain time—*before*, that is, the coded document could be got to him. You see, if it *was* got to him, and his mind was in working order, he might take weeks to do the decoding or he might take no more than a few hours. That sort of thing can be, it seems, a highly intuitive business. Well, we regarded Nauze as at risk, of course, even although we didn't realise that the Overcombe hide-out had been spotted. So he wasn't altogether easy to get at. In fact, they didn't get their chance until the eleventh hour—or well past that—and then it was largely a matter of luck. We were waiting for the helicopter to come in—'

'The midnight helicopter that Beadon and Walcot spoke of?'

'No doubt. Nauze had been drinking a bit—we had been instructed we mustn't try to keep him off it altogether—and as a result—'

'He took a gym-shoe to you.'

'Don't be silly. It took him as anxious to show his independence and cunning. He slipped away and went wandering through the grounds just before dawn. And that was the end of him. They pounced, and shot him dead. And it was I, as it happened, who had first tumbled to his making off. I came on the scene while his limbs were still jerking.'

'Christ!' Bobby looked at Susan aghast, and could find no other word to utter. For a moment he felt alarmingly sick—and then merely very cold. 'Go on,' he said. 'That was at Overcombe. We've got to get to Linger.'

'Yes. *They* had to get to Linger. Or, rather, that's quite wrong. They just had to get somewhere. With the body, that is.'

'But why?'

'It's routine, more or less. You dump your corpse at least a hundred miles from where you killed it, and there's always a chance it may never be so much as identified. And you see what put a golf-course in their heads. They could dump the body of Nauze there in such a way that they could themselves make an undisturbed getaway after doing so, while at the same time making quite sure that it would be discovered fairly early in the morning. You remember the dead-line. It *had* to be discovered, if their employers were to be satisfied. No dead Nauze on time, no pay. Well, they had a van. They shoved the body in the back of it, and drove off. I travelled with them.'

'What!' Bobby stared at Susan dumbfounded. He realised that this girl was going to terrify him intermittently
all his life. 'You just went along?'

'It was quite easy. I simply hopped in with the corpse.
For one thing, it seemed essential to make sure that it *was*
a corpse. Not that I know quite what I'd have done if the
poor man had been faintly alive. And remember that this
was a shattering defeat. *Some* sort of reply was essential.
To go for the buggy-ride was a reply of sorts. Besides, I
was assisted by the marvels of modern science.'

'Just what do you mean by that?'

'I had my walkie-talkie. It's something we're never
allowed to move without. As soon as the van got going,
I could murmur into it quite safely. So I wasn't exactly in-
communicado. The real difficulty was in keeping track of
where we were. But occasionally I managed to see a sign-
post in the headlights of another car. And within an hour
we had been picked up and were being tailed.'

'A car, a caravan, and two men!'

'Just that—and one of the men rather high up. So I'd
become just an attendant lord again. If you think the sub-
sequent conduct of Her Britannic Majesty's secret agents
absurd, you can reflect that it wasn't me who was giving
the orders.'

'I don't know whether they were absurd, but I do sus-
pect that I myself was treated a little hardly by them.'

'Well, yes—that's true. My own difficulty, of course, was
getting out of the van without being spotted, but I managed it when our bearded friends halted to make a pre-
liminary survey of the course. I had to do a bit of rather
cautious walking after that, if I wasn't to give myself
away. But I didn't need to hurry, since the control of the
operation was now in other hands. And that's how it was
that I came on you just when I did. The killers of Nauze
had been allowed to drive off—which no doubt seems very
shocking to your lay mind. But there was, as you'll gather,

method of a sort in that particular piece of madness. My colleagues were just finishing up making an innocent business of an early-morning cup of tea by the roadside. And there, gaping at the bunker, was a perfectly gorgeous young man.'

'True,' Bobby said. 'Continue.'

'By what was obviously sheer coincidence this young oaf—'

'Hey!'

'This young Apollo showed signs of being in a position to identify the body. I doubted whether that would be a good idea. We're taught, you see, to keep the outside world *out*. You understand? At least I had to invent delaying tactics. So I got you off to the club-house, and then beat it for the car. Susan Danbury—or 009 or somebody—reporting for orders. You know what happened then.'

'The whole precious age of you made off with the body, and even left that bunker nicely raked over. I'm damned if I can see why.'

'It's quite fair you should have a mild sense of grievance.' Susan was amused. 'But surely you *can* see why? Nauze duly killed, and body left in bunker on Linger golf-course. That's what the engaging couple would report. But no body is ever found there—nor is Nauze, dead or alive. They may be making the whole thing up, just in the hope of getting their pay. Uncertainty and confusion are sown in the minds of the enemy, and so we have made the best of a very poor show. We're often doing that.' Susan sipped her coffee. 'Are you beginning to come clear?'

'If you *call* it clear.' Bobby broke off. He might have been trying to find some small point of sanity in the middle of all this dangerous nonsense. 'It must have been quite a shock to you,' he said with satisfaction, 'when I turned up at Overcombe. I must say you carried it off well in old Hartsilver's hut. But you had to produce some shocking lies afterwards.'

'It was a little awkward, I admit. And it was rather nice when I got orders this afternoon to let you in on it all.'

'Just how did that happen?'

'Something to do with your father.'

'My father!' Bobby didn't sound at all pleased. 'What had my father to do with it?'

'He seems to be somebody very important. And he tumbled, I imagine, to the kind of affair this is. The hush-hush aspect of it would tell him at once, if he happens to be clued up in these matters. And he seems to have guessed, perfectly correctly, that you were pushing in on the situation in a dangerous state of ignorance and innocence. So he made no bones about getting on the blower to M. himself.' Susan paused. 'Or even,' she added solemnly, 'to M's boss. No doubt he raised firm but gentle hell—the way top people know how to do.'

'Would it have been with that dan⸱⸱⸱⸱⸱⸱⸱⸱⸱⸱⸱⸱⸱rs?'

'Might be. Anyway, the report ⸱⸱⸱⸱⸱⸱⸱⸱⸱⸱⸱⸱⸱ meaning, conscientious, reliable, and likely to be ⸱⸱⸱ competent in a rough house—and therefore to be ⸱⸱ cruited forthwith. Temporary appointment and no pay. Still, Bobby Appleby's dream comes true. He's 008.'

'And now he's going to ask for his bill.' Bobby signed to the waiter. 'Let's hope no pay doesn't mean no expenses.'

CHAPTER ELEVEN

OUTSIDE, THE NIGHT was very dark.

Bobby found this unexpected. He wondered why. He also found it rather menacing and sinister. He wondered about that too. But the feeling of unexpectedness was easily explained. He had a well-developed sense of times and seasons, and unconsciously he was prepared to step into moonlight. Those wild nocturnal events on Linger golf-course had transacted themselves just before the full of the moon. That had been in the small hours of Tuesday. It was late on Friday night now, and a splendid moon— Solo Hoobin's moon—must definitely be on duty. And so, of course, must be the punctual and untiring stars in their courses. But nothing was on view. Above the Three Feathers and its puny festal lights the heavens were overcast. *Come, seeling night* ...

That the darkness felt far from benign was also explicable. Like hundreds, indeed thousands, of agreeably circumstanced young men around England that evening, he had been entertaining a girl to dinner in a country pub— differing from the majority, it might be said, only in that his intentions were strictly honourable. But this, of course, was to neglect the wider context of the occasion. The girl was a working girl, and she had elected to earn her keep within a small lurid world in which people got great chunks of their heads blown off ... Bobby recalled reading a French *roman policier* with the engagingly simple title of *Danger!* (One can't dwell with *la nouvelle écriture* all the time.) And *danger* was hovering all around now.

'Do you know about *danger*?' he heard himself ask.

'*Danger?* Do you mean danger?'

'Yes and no.' They were now more or less groping their way to Bobby's car. 'When one was a lover within the mediaeval code of Courtly Love—'

'*L'amour courtois.*'

'Yes. I see you didn't leave Somerville or wherever without the ghost of an education. When one was that sort of lover, one thought of oneself as within one's lady's *danger*. It was a relationship, really, between a vassal and his lord. Within the code, the lady's the lord, of course, and the lover's the vassal. The lord (or mistress) can require the vassal (or lover) to do his stuff—to be modestly competent, for example, in that rough house.'

'Yes?'

'In requital, the vassal (or lover) is entitled to enjoy the favour of his lord (or mistress). And the reciprocal relationship between the two is called *danger*. See?'

'Do see. *Danger* is definitely on.'

The head-swimming business assailed Bobby Appleby again.

'Pray God,' he said, 'I'm not too madly drunk on you to drive this bloody car.'

Cars are best at night. Their engines seem to take on a new smoothness and power. One seems to be a better driver, too. The darkness parted before the speed of Bobby and Susan, and closed again behind them.

'We're going back to Overcombe,' Bobby said. 'Is that right?'

'Yes. Quite right. I've had my holiday.'

'Listen, Susan. What I don't understand, really, is what might be called the continuing situation. Nauze is dead, and will solve no more conundrums about anti-ballistic missiles, or anything else. So just what's going on?'

'We're lying low.'

'Are those bearded chaps lying low?'

'They puzzle me rather, I'm bound to say. I've told you

163

they're just low-class killers. And they killed Nauze, all right. They ought really to have had their pay, too. Because of the leak.'

'The leak?'

'It seems we didn't get away, after all, with the picture of Bobby Appleby as just imagining things in that bunker. There was a bit in a paper. And the other side—the bearded chaps' bosses, that is—were smart enough to winkle a confirmatory statement out of the local police. So these two chaps ought to have cleared out by now. Incidentally, Bobby, I've only your word for it that they *haven't* cleared out. It was you who saw them when you were coming back from your prowl to the Great Smithy. It was you who saw one of them peering at us through that dining-room door.'

'Bobby Appleby imagining things, after all?'

'Well, no. But it's a puzzle. Where can they be hanging out? We've had the whole countryside combed in vain for the slightest trace of them. And *why* should they be hanging out? Perhaps—'

'That's the one I want answered. Why should that fellow have peered in on us? What are they after *still*?'

'They can't have tumbled to Hartsilver. It's just not possible.'

It was suddenly clear to Bobby that Susan was wrong. She was too close up to the thing. He himself had arrived from outside, with perhaps a certain power of fresh assessment. And what seemed not possible to Susan seemed not impossible to him.

'This document,' he said. 'About missiles being taught to hit missiles that are being taught to hit missiles that are being taught to hit you. You know it's absolute nonsense, don't you?'

'These things exist.'

'But they're just something other than human life. We mustn't bother our heads with them—any more than with the fact that one day San Francisco is bound more or less to vanish in another earthquake.'

'What utter rot! Earthquakes are God. Missiles are men. And likely to leave mere genocide standing.'

'Well, yes. We will all go together when we go—'

'Every Hottentot and every Eskimo. But that doesn't mean—' Susan broke off, and laughed softly in the darkness. Knowing the same song had pleased them. 'Bobby, what on earth are we talking about?'

'That missile document.'

'Yes. Well, it's in London, being worried at by a whole college of cryptographers. But I photographed it first.'

'Off your own bat?'

'Off my own bat.'

'I like a girl to have a certain nerve. Would the photograph be an attractive proposition to the bearded characters and their employers?'

'Not to their *original* employers. There's obviously nothing in it that *they* don't know. *Their* concern was to prevent our getting hold of the thing, or cracking its code once we had got it. But it's beginning to seem possible to me'—Susan was suddenly speaking rather slowly—'that your bearded characters may be thinking of *changing* employers. A lot of these affairs are three-cornered, you know.'

'Three-cornered?'

'Three Great Powers, each playing for its own hand. Or four, at times.'

'So they might like your photograph—to sell to some other concern?'

'Yes—but they'd like it much more if it was no longer in code, but already in clear.'

'If some Nauze had done his stuff on it?'

'Yes.'

'Susan, you said something about Hartsilver—that he was trying to do what Nauze might have done. It's he who has your photograph? He's working on it—with everything Nauze taught him? And that's your private gamble?'

'We're taught to take an initiative now and then.'

'But it won't be too good if this goes wrong?'

'No, it won't.'

Bobby drove in silence for the rest of the way back to Overcombe. He hadn't drunk much, but he didn't drive fast. This was less because of road-mindedness than because of quite a lot going on in his head. Susan must be—or must have been—incredibly good at this MI5 stuff or she wouldn't, at her age, have got as far as she had with it. At the same time, it was an outrageous walk of life for any girl who was even approximately like Susan. He was entirely clear about that. Doing very, very dangerous things —yes. Tiptop rock-climbing, for instance. Flying solo round the world. Or sailing ditto. Or working way-out in hazardous research with lethal substances. All that. But this, no.

A certain grim fastidiousness hadn't much impeded the career of Appleby Senior in the field of low life and criminal practice. Deep down, Bobby had inherited the same slant of mind. This did mean (he judged) that he wouldn't be a terribly good authentic oo8. But that was irrelevant. The point was that—at a crunch—Susan Danbury wouldn't be all that good as oo—and—whatever. She too had disabilities, although they might not be the same disabilities as those of Appleby Junior. This business of chancing her hand with old Hartsilver: it was imaginative and courageous, but it wasn't, in the last analysis, the winning thing in a world in which cautious cunning was all. To clear this up and yank Susan out was the purpose for which the gods had conducted him to that bunker.

He could, of course, simply turn the car round and drive to some remote part of England. He had a rather horrified intuition that Susan would submit. But it would be as a girl submits to her ravisher. It would be a solution of the situation transacting itself in very deep and dark places indeed. Not on, he told himself. Definitely not on.

'Do you know,' he said cheerfully, as they turned into the school drive, 'that I don't know where or how Hartsilver lives? But, wherever it is, we'll go and tuck him up now.'

'Yes.'

Bobby slowed down yet further. He found this response uncommunicative. But at least—he noticed—it was conveyed in the word which Susan had now rather frequently availed herself of.

'Speak up,' he said. 'You've set him to this task, and you're convinced that nobody is thinking about him. But at least he ought to be under some sort of guard. Is he? Or is he a lonely old man, isolated in some remote cottage in the grounds? Over to you.'

'Turn left.'

At rather short notice, Bobby turned left. He remembered that there had always been two or three lanes of this sort, running from the main drive to cottages inhabited by members of the staff at Overcombe. But he didn't remember this one, and supposed it must be more or less new. It was a winding green tunnel, and his headlights probed it cautiously.

'Far down?' he asked.

'By the river. You're right that it's fairly remote. But he's not alone. There's one of our men keeping an eye on him. Not obtrusively, I hope. He's supposed to be repairing the swimming-pool, and to have been given the spare bedroom in Hartsilver's cottage. His name's Leaver.'

'Ominous. We'll hope he hasn't left him. Here we are.'

Hartsilver's house seemed to be a small bungalow. But the sky was still entirely obscured, and it wasn't possible to see much. The murmur of the little river bounding Overcombe on the west could just be heard, and above this

—curiously sharp—the croaking of frogs. A faint complex scent hung in the air: honeysuckle, Bobby thought, and perhaps a nicotine-plant. There was a low light in a porch; and, to one side of this, more light filtered through a curtained window. They climbed from the car and walked towards the door.

'Roses round it,' Bobby said. 'And listen.'

Music was filtering from the cottage into the night—canned but stereophonic. Bobby, who was not musical, had a vague notion it was the Fifth Symphony. If it was, he didn't, somehow, like the sound of this particular bit. Perhaps it was where E. M. Forster says that goblins start walking quietly over the universe from end to end. If that was so, there would presently be an interlude with elephants dancing. But the main point was that old Hartsilver appeared to be having a quiet cultural evening.

So for a moment it seemed to Bobby that they were on a fool's errand, and even that they had better, perhaps, clear out. And then with Beethoven's celebrated composition (if it was indeed that) there was blended another sound. It wasn't a sound that could claim the remotest logical relationship to the matter in hand. It was nothing more, in fact, than the faint rattle of a train far away in the dark. But then the train whistled.

The whistle was not of the sort to which Bobby—long ago in his well-appointed and night-light-lit night-nursery —had moderately thrilled: the old-fashioned steam-engine kind of whistle, which might have been emanating from a perfectly ordinary dragon. This whistle didn't rise and fall on an indrawn and out-going breath (accompanied by fire—a small and lurid flame against the sky). This was the mechanical and uniform note of a Diesel-engine—or not uniform only because borne onward into a farther dark at eighty miles an hour. Most irrationally, it alerted Bobby now.

There was another waft of scent. This time it was from

168

the roses, for he had stepped inside the porch, getting Susan behind him. He felt the scratch and prick of a thorn across the back of his hand, and realised that he was reaching for the door-handle rather than searching for a knocker or a bell. Hartsilver seemed not very tidy in his gardening. The music was still going on, and the scent came to him as if mixed up with it. Something moved at his touch.

'Door's ajar,' he said.

'Go in.'

'But it won't open further. I'm shoving against something.'

'Then shove. But not too hard.'

He shoved, and squeezed through. A little light came with him from the porch behind. A little more slanted from a half-open door to one side. He looked down at his feet.

'Don't come in,' he said—sharply and instinctively.

But Susan was already beside him. They had stood rather like this before—side by side, viewing a body. Susan bent over this one.

'Leaver,' she said.

CHAPTER TWELVE

THERE WAS A moment's silence. Or rather, between Bobby and Susan there was that, and at the same time the cottage was full of what seemed a deafening din. Beethoven was winding things up. With vast roarings of a superhuman joy.

Bobby looked at the half-open door through which the music came, and felt a sharp pricking down his spine. He fancied, in a split second of mere muddle, that it was the roses round the door again; that some untended thorny spray had reached out and stroked him. Then he heard himself talking sense.

'His body blocked the outer door. Unless there's a back entrance, nobody can have—'

'There is. And there are windows.' Susan made his remark seem not sensible after all. 'But I think he crawled here.' She was again bending over the body—if not professionally, at least composedly enough. 'He's been killed, all right. Stabbed. But not instantly. Left dying. And he tried to crawl out.' She spoke jerkily. 'Find Hartsilver.'

The music stopped.

Bobby's body had tautened, and instinctively he knew that Susan's had too. It was as if they were both for a fraction of time under the delusive persuasion that, failing some immediate human agency, music *can't* stop. Then Bobby acted. He turned, and made for the room the music had been coming from. Three paces took him through the door and into it. It was quite a large room, or at least it seemed so in terms of the general scale of the place. Although it was lined with books, there was enough space to give the record-player a chance. The only picture was a small one over the fireplace: an unassuming reproduction of Dürer's 'St Jerome in his Study'. Dürer must be Hartsilver's favourite artist—if Hartsilver, Bobby suddenly reflected, was properly to be spoken of as having a favourite anything any longer.

Bobby looked around him, and caught his breath. He had never before been in a room that could be described as having been broken up or wrecked. (His Oxford college was one at which smashing people's rooms had ceased to be an accepted form of social intercourse.) He didn't like the look of the thing now—not even the look of the untouched record-player, with the aid of which Beethoven must have continued to plumb the recesses of human experience throughout whatever lurid events had been transacting themselves. There was no sign of Hartsilver—of Hartsilver whether dead or alive. But there was a sofa, a desk, a long curtain drawn across a window-space. Bobby hurried round, peering.

'Nothing.' Susan was in the doorway, and he spoke as he turned to her. 'No sign of him.'

'Nor anywhere else in the place.' She must have made a rapid tour. 'Too late. We lose again. Or I do.'

He looked at her in horror, and then back at the room.

'A ghastly mess,' he said. 'Ransacked.'

'Not that. Precisely not that.' She was looking round with an eye more expert than his. 'Not a search. Just a struggle. Leaver put up a fight. Hartsilver too, perhaps.'

'What have they done with him? Where can he be now?'

'They didn't have to hunt for anything.' Susan had ignored the questions. She was speaking very quietly. 'No drawers tugged open. No books pulled out. Carpet not hauled back. So they probably just picked up what they wanted from that desk.'

'Your photostat, or whatever it's called?'

'Well, that—yes. And perhaps something else.'

'You mean Hartsilver's successful decoding of it as well?'

'Not exactly that. If they'd got *that*, Hartsilver would still be here. Dead too, I suppose. Say, just what looked like a promising start.'

'They've taken him away—alive?'

'Yes.' Susan's voice had gone momentarily toneless and flat. 'I'm afraid that's my appreciation of the situation.'

'If way to the Better there be, it exacts a full look at the Worst.'

'Bobby, don't be literary—for God's sake.'

'But it's true. And the worst is just this: that your inspired little plan has landed this harmless old creature in a nasty spot. They'll hold him till he finishes the job. Perhaps twisting bits and pieces of him from time to time just to hurry him up.'

'Bobby, please!'

'No—not Bobby, please. Just plain fact, and we're both equally responsible. Face it, and we begin to feel a fraction better. Is there a telephone in this place?'

'No.'

'Are there more Leavers anywhere in the immediate vicinity?'

'No. He was the only one left me. But we had a whole group scouring the countryside for those two killers, and it appeared certain they'd cleared out. Then you meet them in broad daylight. We have to work on that.'

'Won't they be more or less on their own? I mean that their action only makes sense if they're preparing to swop paymasters. You explained that to me. It's no good their taking this decoded thing to the people who instructed them to liquidate Nauze. Those people *have* this gen. They're now out for something they can flog to a third party—or government. That means, surely, that they're free-lancers just at the moment. It makes them less formidable. We just find them, and I batter their brains out.'

'Wouldn't that be rather drastic?' Susan contrived to smile bleakly.

'Not in the least. They've made themselves a nuisance to you. So at least I'll have them howling for mercy.' Bobby looked at his watch. 'But the first thing is to stop being free-lances ourselves. You must report the current situation to your bosses. That's why I asked about a telephone. After that, we *can* put in a spell going it alone. I've an idea, as a matter of fact.'

'An idea?' She looked at him round-eyed.

'A wild one, but an idea, all the same. I wish we had a gun.'

'But we have. Leaver's. He never managed to draw it, however hard he fought. And they didn't pause to collect it. I've just found it under him. Rather bloody, but that won't impair the works.'

'Good.' Those last words, it seemed to Bobby, had come from Susan with a rather forlorn defiance. There must be a limit, in this sort of thing, to what any girl could take. 'I'll pocket it.'

'*I'll* pocket it. I'm taught about such things.'

'So am I. Officers are still supposed to carry revolvers. They're to persuade other ranks to keep moving in the right direction, I suppose. So we were taught to handle them in the O.T.C. And now we'll be off.'

'Off? Where to?'

'We're going up on the downs. But there's a telephone at the cross roads at the foot of Lark Hill. That's where you'll report from.'

'Bobby—'

'Pick up your trailing skirts, girl, and run.'

'Well?' Bobby said ten minutes later, when Susan had come out of the telephone kiosk.

'We'll be thick on the ground in not much over an hour.'

'*We*? What the hell! You don't mean it takes over an hour to rustle up a bunch of local coppers?'

'Bobby, dear, my people wouldn't think of having *them* in. We keep ourselves to ourselves—M. & Co. do.'

'Very well.' Bobby swore robustly as he let in the clutch. 'It's still just two against two—or so we're reckoning. But —do you know?—while you were on the blower I had an odd notion we were being spied on. I wish the sky would clear, and give the moon a chance. It may soon. There's a breeze coming up. It may get those clouds moving.'

'What do you mean—being spied on?' Susan spoke sharply.

'Flitting forms in the murk—that kind of thing. This light on the instrument-panel was a bit bright. I ought to have turned down the rheostat. A sitting target, I'd have been. Or at least easy to identify. You too, for that matter, inside that glass telephone-affair. Let's get on.'

'Bobby, is this a hunch?'

'A hunch? My father, who has shoved in his oar on me —' Bobby broke off. 'Pretty usefully, to be fair. You and I might have been at cross-purposes a lot longer, I suppose, if he hadn't started throwing his weight around. What was I saying? *He* sometimes has hunches. But I don't call this a hunch, quite. It's straight topography.'

'Topography?'

'They were surprised, you know, when I bobbed up on them. It was because I'd been sunning myself behind a bank—and I'd jumped up, and there I was, at quite close quarters, looking down on them. But *I* was surprised too. I was more puzzled than I realised at the time. For there was just nowhere they could have come from. Except out of the earth. And that, of course, is it. It's a weird explanation. But we must accept it, since there just isn't another. They've treated themselves to a hide-out in the Great Smithy.'

'It would explain there being no trace of them in any-thing that can be called a human habitation—or a cattle-shed—for miles around. But it doesn't quite make sense. There are always likely to be a few tourists and walkers and people peering in there. Almost every day, surely, at this time of year. It's quite a famous archaeological site—one of the most notable chambered tombs in the country.'

'True enough.' They were now half-way up Lark Hill. And suddenly Bobby had slowed, stopped, switched off his lights. 'The moon!' he said.

And there it certainly was: Solo's orb. As Bobby thought of it in this way, he momentarily felt a long way from home. This, of course was absurd. Or it was absurd in rela-tion to himself, but not absurd in relation to Susan. He thought he'd better get this clear now.

'Listen,' he said. 'I'd like to send you home.'

'Thank you very much.'

'Wait. I'd like to send you home, and run up and finish off this business myself.'

'You're the most cocksure—'

'I said wait. I realise you started this Hartsilver episode, and have to see it through. All right. But that's the finish. I'm not going to be married to Susan the Secret Service Girl. I'm a plain unromantic man.'

There was a long silence.

'Have said,' Susan said. 'It looks as if it may be quite a nice moon.'

This was true. The moon had, indeed, only taken a quick look at them, and vanished again from direct view. But elsewhere there must be a larger break in the cloud, since ahead the whole line of the down was defining itself in a faint radiance.

'Yes,' Bobby said. 'But I don't know whether it's going to be useful, or just a bit of an embarrassment. And I think we'd better walk from here on. We could drive slowly up to the top without lights, I suppose. But on a night like this the sound of a car carries for miles. There's a torch in the glove-box.'

They began to walk up the rest of Lark Hill. The long crest of the down, already an immemorial highway when first glimpsed by the legionaries of Caesar, now showed dark against a rapidly clearing sky.

'There it is.' Bobby had halted briefly to point. Ahead of them and to the right, the natural flow of the chalk, calligraphic as a brush-stroke by some Chinese master, rose abruptly, ran on a low parallel, dropped again. The Great Smithy was like a gigantic caterpillar slumbering on the sky-line. 'About a mile away.'

'Bobby, it still seems a pretty long shot to me. Too public. People go poking in, as I said.'

'Have you poked in?'

'Too busy.'

'Well, I remember it from long ago, and I've read about it since. It's megalithic—which means chiefly that it's a kind of long gallery, walled and roofed in enormous stones. The earth and turf one sees are only a kind of top-dressing. There are some of these things where all that has been washed away. Lanyon Quoit in Cornwall, for example. It's like what furniture-shops call a coffee-table. But you'd be putting down your cup on a stone slab three-feet thick. The Smithy's basically like that. It's also what's called a chambered tomb, as you said. Think of it as a buried railway-carriage, with a lot of compartments on a corridor—all neatly buried underground. Or something roughly like that.' Bobby paused on this wealth of comparison. 'I'm not all that certain about it. But I do remember there was only one chamber excavated in my time, and I think a bit more has been done recently. It's my idea that these chaps may be using some of these further burrowings for their temporary hide-out. They could probably be disguised easily enough.'

They walked rapidly on, in spite of the steep gradient.

176

The night was quite still. When they put up a pheasant by the road-side, the whirr and clatter with which it rocketed away was like a sudden burst from a quick-firing gun close to their feet. They had found they could move without using the torch. Bobby, with Susan's hand in his, concentrated on keeping to the middle of the faintly visible track. Susan kept a look-out on a wide arc around them. It was she who stopped and pointed next.

'A light,' she said. 'Moving.'

'I don't see it.'

'It comes and goes. Flickers. If the Smithy's noon, it's at about four o'clock.'

'Yes.' The bearing had taken Bobby's glance where his right shoulder had just been. 'I think it's a torch.'

'Then it's somebody being less careful than us. Is there a track over there?'

'Yes—a very steep one. It's the most direct way up. We used to call it the Scramble.'

'Then there's a spot of scrambling going on.'

'Lovers, perhaps. Or a shepherd.' Bobby marched on. 'Or—let's face it—an unsuspected reinforcement of bearded men. It can't be your lot yet.'

'No,' Susan said calmly. 'Not by a long way.'

On a Field Day with the Corps—Bobby told himself, thinking back to schooldays—he might have been told to capture the Great Smithy. That would have been by daylight. The exercise would have been all about taking cover in various improbable ways—and, of course, about one lot of chaps providing covering fire for another lot of chaps. All that firing blank had been great fun—even when one of the pros on the job came up and told you you were all dead. But at the yearly Camp it might have been a nocturnal affair, and so approximately like this. There had been Very lights and star-shells to add a little verisimilitude to those occasions and again a great deal of blazing away.

But any blazing away done tonight would certainly not be with blank cartridges.

Bobby had gone over the dead Leaver's revolver with care. His hand was on the butt of it in the pocket of his jacket now. For they had come to their first critical place: the point at which the prehistoric track—venerable artery of commerce, war, migration—upon the verge of which the Great Smithy stood, crossed the little-frequented modern road they had been following. Here, turning to the right, they had to take to the turf. So far, hedges, telegraph-poles, post-and-rail fences had marched on one or the other side of them—giving some illusion, at least, of screening them from hostile view. Now there was only this immemorial arterial road. It was bounded on either side, no doubt, by some miserable strand of wire. But (in this struggling moonlight, at least) its breadth seemed like that of a motorway of the sort that swept you out of Seattle or Chicago. It was a very unprotected place.

CHAPTER THIRTEEN

THEY WERE BEFORE the Great Smithy—facing the giant caterpillar head-on through a scattering of beeches. And the moon had suddenly appeared high above them, seemingly unchallenged in the heavens. Almost as if at the flick of a switch, it had reduced to nonsense the notion of a stealthy nocturnal approach. There was one further clump of trees to which a dash for concealment could be made. But after that they would be confronting a sinister no man's land of bare turf. If caught there by an enemy securely under cover, their position would be as ugly as could be.

'They've made rather a suburban job of it,' Bobby whispered. He was moved not by any particular wish to be disrespectful to the Ministry of Works or to the learned persons known as the Curators of Ancient Monuments, but rather by an obscure feeling that flippant words steady the nerves. And the trim little brick path did seem out of context. It led straight from a neat gate in a perimeter fence to the Smithy's entrance. The entrance was a narrow slit, and impenetrably dark. It was like a gash in the conscious mind through which one gazed into the recesses of the anarchic id. On either side of it—casually present, it seemed, rather than set there for any ritual purpose—were two of the great sarsen stones which lay about the surface of the down like the abandoned tennis-balls of departed gods.

It might be quicker to get through the gate than over the fence. The gate—Bobby saw—had one of those notices expensively manufactured in cast-iron which the Ancient Monuments people seemed to be particularly fond of. It

179

no doubt told you that you were liable to prosecution if you started bashing the Smithy around, or succumbed to the temptation to scratch your name on it. Bobby had a sudden odd fantasy which came and went in an instant of time: he was crouching by the gate, and a bearded character took a pot-shot at him from that sinister orifice ahead, and the bullet slammed into the notice and thereby saved his life.

This at least made him wonder whether he should draw his own revolver. He also wondered whether he ought to hand it to Susan. Perhaps he had exaggerated his familiarity with this form of small-arm. Probably people in Susan's peculiar line of business, whether male or female, were required to put in an hour's practice with such things once a week. And he and Susan weren't at the moment in a position in which merely conventional notions of what is proper to one sex or the other ought to be too rigidly applied. Bobby wanted to hold on to the thing himself, nevertheless.

'Keep that gun ready,' Susan said. 'And listen.'

For a full minute they stood immobile, straining their ears. There wasn't a sound. Or certainly there wasn't a sound from the Smithy—any more than there was the faintest gleam of light from it. But Bobby realised how easy it was, in a situation like this, to start imagining things. He could have sworn that—as with the poet Wordsworth upon an occasion of similar alarm—there were low breathings coming after him.

'Sounds,' he whispered, 'of undistinguishable motion.'

'Steps almost as silent as the turf they trod.' For an instant Susan's hand took his; she had accepted this too as an aid to keeping one's nerve. 'And low breathings coming after us. But I expect it's sheep. Bobby, we'll go through the gate. And then each make for one of those two trees on the left. You take the one nearest the path.'

They broke cover and ran. The gate opened with a loud creak. Bobby told himself that one would keep it that way if one had set up house in the recesses of the Great Smithy and wanted due notice of inconvenient intrusion. But at least nothing happened, and they gained their trees. But now they were separated by some yards, and a whisper would have to be something of a stage-whisper if it were to carry between them. And again Bobby seemed to hear stealthy movement. He looked all round, and in particular back among the beeches for the forms of straying animals—sheep or even cattle—which ought to be clearly enough visible in this light. He could see nothing that suggested the faintest movement. And now his fancy took another undisciplined bound—so that what his eye sought was human forms, prone and creeping: here the sheen of a naked torso and there the glint of the tip of a spear. Such carryings-on had been all the go up here through millennia which showed the armies of Hadrian and Alfred, of Harold and William, as but of yesterday. Perhaps some ghostly re-enactment of ancient battle, foray, surprise, regularly accompanied the full of Solo's moon.

Instinctively he had crouched down, and he wondered whether it would be any use actually to get on his belly and crawl. He didn't think so. On the contrary, indeed, it was now his business to stand up and be counted. For if his guess was right, if the bearded men with their prisoner were really somewhere concealed within the Smithy, then the only way to cope—short of waiting passively for help —was to take the place by storm. Of course they *ought* to wait for help—help which might now be arriving in less than half an hour. No other behaviour could honestly be called rational. But if the bearded men had taken the risk and trouble of bringing Hartsilver up here, it certainly wasn't for any purpose that could be called a pretty one. They had only to know, or even to fancy they knew, that the old man had the solution of that idiotic code virtually at his command, and they might treat him in a fashion too barbarous for decent contemplation. In short, the only choice was to rush the beggars.

Bobby's right hand already grasped the revolver. He put his left hand in his pocket and brought out the torch. It would be needed the instant he was beyond that dark portal. He looked down at his shoes, and toed off each in turn. He could run quite silently on the brick path that way. He glanced at Susan behind her tree, and saw that she was kicking off her shoes too. Which meant he hadn't an instant to spare. This Hartsilver business had hit her hard. She was quite capable of taking the lead, and of dashing into the Smithy unarmed. Or she might take it into her head to shout and to run nowhere in particular—this by way of drawing the enemy's fire.

Bobby was running now—running as he had never run down a touch-line in his young athletic life. But even as he ran he noticed something at his feet. The moon, still doing its stuff, had cast there the shadow of a dancing human head. Susan was very close behind him indeed.

Nothing. Silence. Darkness. Darkness cut only by the beam of his own torch. Chill. And a smell that wasn't quite of earth—but rather of unbelievable antiquity. If unbelievable antiquity can smell.

Swiftly he cast the beam into the first chamber. It lay on his left hand. Nothing was revealed, and he hurried on. It was a surprisingly long way to a second aperture, and when he reached it and raked it there was only a small empty space. He went further, and stopped dead. He had to do this. He was confronting a door. A door is not a common appurtenance of a megalithic chambered tomb.

It was a stout wooden door—with a couple of bolts of the kind that can be secured with a padlock. But the door was slightly ajar. And it moved as they looked at it. But only through the smallest angle. Perhaps a faint draught—

a sighing to and fro of faint currents of air—was at play in this gloomy place.

There was nothing out of the way about it. This came to Bobby almost at once. It hadn't been imported by wandering Slavonic personages with beards. The Ministry of Works—which one thought of as simply a bowler-hatted gentleman carrying an umbrella—had caused it to be installed out of a provident care for the safety of those members of the archaeologically-minded public who might penetrate as far as this into the *arcanum* of the Great Smithy. Beyond this point the going was still hazardous. Only, the bowler-hatted gentleman had forgotten his padlock. Or perhaps it was still upon requisition from another Government Department.

'It looks like a mare's nest, wouldn't you say?' For the first time for what seemed an aeon, Susan spoke confidently and aloud. 'No go, in fact. We must start again.'

'No doubt.' Bobby's eye was on the faintly swaying door. It had explained itself to him in a flash, but he didn't like it, all the same. He told himself that it was simply a final test of nerve. He could creep towards it. Or he could do as he had been doing, and make a dash at it. He made a dash. This time, Susan was only inches behind him.

A small chamber, very void indeed. And a *cul-de-sac*. So that was the end of this wild-goose chase. As Susan said, they must start again.

The chill air with its queer smell—its neolithic smell—stirred behind Bobby and Susan. The Ministry's useful door had closed behind them. They heard a bolt going home.

'The first chamber must have another off it,' Bobby said quietly. 'They were lurking there. *Plus* Hartsilver, poor bastard.' He hesitated. 'Susan, I'm sorry.'

'Shut up—Bobby, my own darling.' Susan had *meant* Shut up. She was listening intently. 'They're very pro-

183

fessional,' she said, approvingly and coldly. 'They don't even bother to gloat.'

The silence continued for a long time—or what seemed a long time. And then they heard an evil sound. It was a very evil sound indeed—a long, low moan of agony.

'That's it,' Bobby said. 'Off that first chamber there's quite a big second one. They're operating there.' He paused for a moment. 'I've still got this bloody gun. But it's not much use through stone three-feet thick. It may be useful, I suppose, if we're left here to die of thirst.'

'Don't be silly, Bobby. In twenty minutes they'll be here. By the helicopter. And dozens of them by car half an hour later.'

'Bad half-hour for Hartsilver.'

'He has to take his chance. Just keep that gun ready, Bobby. They may try some funny stuff.'

Bobby kept the gun ready. Through the red rage raised in him by the muted sound of another groan, he told himself—obstinately and as a kind of point of sanity—that Susan Danbury was his girl. That—if they both died like rats thirty seconds from now.

'008.'

Bobby stiffened. His ears weren't deceiving him.

'Sir. 008. Is that a torch? Put it out.'

Bobby flicked off the torch. There was only absolute darkness.

'Can you see, 008 or Sir?' The voice was unmistakably Beadon's. 'There *are* all those chinks, you know. The Smithy's tumbling to bits, really. All those enormous stones. But a good heave would shift them.'

'I don't think so, Beadon. Not quite.' Bobby spoke very softly. 'But you're right about the chinks. I'm beginning to see them.'

'What shall we do, Sir—008, I mean?'

184

'Who's we? You and Walcot?'

'No, Sir. The whole school. We thought that might be the best thing. When you told us about meeting those men near the Smithy.'

'You were quite right. But I hope Dr Gulliver will agree.'

'We left him a note, as a matter of fact. It seemed the decent thing—poor agitated old soul.'

'No wonder Susan and I heard sounds of undistinguishable motion. They've bolted us in.'

'In the place beyond that door? We know it. We come exploring here. Just the bolts, do you think?'

'That's my impression, Beadon.'

'Then Weedy can do it.'

'Weedy?'

'Weedy Green, Sir. He can snake anywhere. Would those men be in the big room—the one off the first one?'

'Yes.'

'Then there's a kind of threshold. Did you see it, Sir? Raised more than a foot. Weedy can snake past it, and get at that bolt. May we send him in, oo8?'

'No!' Susan said.

'Yes, Beadon.' Weedy Green, Bobby told himself, was very small. But he was an English gentleman (and all that) in the making. Hartsilver being the stake, Weedy had better have a go. 'Weedy's to creep in, draw the bolt, and skip in here as fast as he can. Then you'll hear a shot. Got that? A single shot. Is Walcot there?'

'Sir!' This was Walcot's voice.

'Confirm, Walcot.'

'A single shot, Sir. oo8, that is.'

'Right. The moment you hear that shot, all hell is to break loose. Understand? The whole school.'

'O.K.' Walcot's voice was low but triumphant. 'Leave it to Beadon and me. We'll promise to leather the bottom off any man who doesn't yell like mad.'

'Carry on, Beadon and Walcot.'

For a long half-minute Bobby listened. There wasn't a sound.

'Susan,' he whispered, 'of course this kid Green is first priority. The moment the door opens—if it does—I go through, and cover the entrance of the chamber where these bastards have got Hartsilver. You take Green's hand and follow. And you don't stop till you're in the open air. Then I'll evacuate the place at gun-point. Right?'

'Right.'

They stood immobile—side by side and in utter darkness. The chinks through which some faint glint of moonlight came didn't amount to letting one see a thing. But Bobby's hand was on the door. And after an age it quivered, faintly creaked, moved on its hinges. Bobby stepped aside, put out a hand to the invisible boy, and gently guided him into Susan's arms.

'I'm going,' he breathed, and glided through the doorway. The revolver was in his right hand. So it was with his left hand—which also held the torch—that he had to feel along the cold stone close by his right shoulder. When it met vacancy, that would be the small, empty chamber. When it felt vacancy again, that would be the antechamber (as it must have been) which he had failed to realise had some further chamber beyond it. Here he would pause. And Susan and the boy called Weedy Green would slip past him.

He had got there, and still there wasn't a sound—so that he wondered whether the enemy, having somehow silenced Hartsilver, were alerted and waiting. Only, there was a light: the faintest filter of light, such as might seep round more than one sharp turn in a constricted space. He felt a breath behind him, waited for some further seconds, and glanced to his left. The other dim light, that from the entrance of the Smithy, was obscured for a moment and then cleared again. Susan and Green were gone. He snapped on the torch, and stepped forward. In the same instant, he fired a single shot behind him. It made a most tremendous row.

He rounded a jutting stone baffle and was in a middle-sized chamber, lit by a low light from a hurricane-lamp. There was a table in the middle, and from either side of this the two bearded men had just sprung to their feet. They might have been interrupted in a quiet little committee-meeting. There were writing-materials on the table, and a couple of glasses, and what appeared to be several bottles of soft drink: one of these was like an old-fashioned ginger-beer bottle—a heavy stoneware thing. Bobby held the men covered, and they were very startled indeed. They well might be. It wasn't merely that this intrusive young man had turned up again within ten minutes of having been safely locked up. It was also that outside the Great Smithy there was a sudden pandemonium of sound which might have betokened the tumultuous release of all the devils in hell. Overcombe was doing well.

But there was no Hartsilver.

'Hartsilver!' Bobby called out—and nothing happened. Bobby felt his finger tremble on the trigger. 'Hartsilver!' he cried out again. And then Hartsilver was before him—risen up from somewhere behind the table: from the floor, perhaps, or a bench or a bed. He didn't look too good, but he might have been looking very much worse. 'Stay still, and listen,' Bobby said. 'You mustn't get between me and either of these men. Skirt the wall of this damned place, and go outside. There's help there.'

And Hartsilver went out. The boys were still yelling like mad. But their moment of immobilising dismay had been achieved, and they could now merely be thought of as enjoying themselves. Left alone with the bearded men—neither of whom had ventured on a menacing movement—Bobby wasn't quite sure of the technique next to be followed. But he remembered that they ought to be told to put their hands up. So he gave this order sharply. It was

187

obeyed at once. There still seemed a bit of an impasse, however. It was almost certain that they both had weapons concealed about their persons, and they would continue a menace until they were expertly disarmed. Bobby was in no doubt of the expertness required. There were two of them, and they were a wily couple. Against them was one man with one gun. It wasn't an occasion for any over-confident movement. The problem was to hold them until armed help arrived.

'I'm going to shove you,' Bobby said, 'where you shoved me—and bolt you in there until you're taken care of. I shall back out, and you will follow at your present distance. Once in the passage, you will back into the far chamber in your turn. If either of you drops an arm, I'll kill him. It will be the only way to deal quickly enough with the other one. Do you understand?'

Both men nodded. The sight of them wagging their beards like that was almost unnervingly grotesque. But Bobby had no inclination not to save up his amusement for a later occasion.

'Listen again,' he said. 'I'm going to count as I back out. You will both take one step, and one only, to each number. *One ... two ... three*—'

'Please!' For the first time, one of the men spoke—and it was very hoarsely. As he did so, he nodded towards the table. 'We may take a drink?'

'You—not the other one—may pick up one bottle as you pass. But keep your hand well away from your body. *Four ... five*—'

The man who had spoken lowered an outstretched arm very gingerly towards the stoneware bottle. In the same instant, Bobby's body did an extraordinary thing. Bobby's body picked up Bobby and dropped him neatly behind that baffle—it was like a great stone buttress—which he had skirted on entering. Or his eye, it might be said, had been in a queer way ahead of his mind. It had been aware that the bottle was not to be picked up, but hurtled towards him.

And then Bobby's ear came into play. It registered a shattering roar. And all his senses signed off at once.

CHAPTER FOURTEEN

Solo Hoobin's moon looked down on Bobby Appleby. Bobby Appleby looked up at Solo Hoobin's moon. He did so without cricking his neck. This was because he was lying flat on his back—quite comfortably, on downland turf.

But, although comfortable, he was obscurely outraged. He endeavoured to struggle into a sitting position—although not, at first, with much success. In fact he sank back again—and so was able to observe a further phenomenon in the heavens. It was a little cluster of coloured lights, and he rather thought that two were steady and one was winking. They were more or less floating down towards him. Bobby supposed that here must be what the newspapers call a UFO—an Unidentified Flying Object. Then the phenomenon began to make quite a familiar noise, and he realised it was a helicopter. He lost interest in the helicopter, and recalled another noise instead. As he did so, his sense of outrage returned with redoubled force, and under the influence of this the power of speech returned to him. His actual words, had he been particularly conscious of them, might have surprised him, since for a robust young man he was very little addicted to coarse language.

'What the bloody hell was that?' Bobby demanded.

'It's called a concussion grenade.' Susan's voice spoke calmly from somewhere above him—perhaps from heaven. 'It hasn't done you much harm.'

'How's Hartsilver?' Bobby's head was clearing rapidly.

'Not much harm either. Of course, suddenly being tortured does rather startle an elderly gentleman. But we were more or less in at the start.'

'Had he solved that idiotic cipher-thing?'

'Absolutely not. It leaves him standing. It was Nauze or nothing, if you ask me.'

'You don't think there's life-or-death in that anti-ballistic stuff, do you?'

'Not if you say not, Bobby. Perhaps you should rest now.'

This brought Bobby scrambling to his feet. Under the serene moon the boys of Overcombe School were sitting around in small groups. Satisfaction was apparent upon the faces of all. Perhaps this was because they had providentially brought provisions with them on their expedition, and they were now in the enjoyment of a midnight collation. Bobby inconsequently wondered whether the bowler-hatted gentleman would send in a force of menial persons to clear up the orange-peel, the lemonade-bottles, and the gaudy wrappings of favoured chocolate confections. And suddenly Bobby became aware of Onslow. Onslow was carrying a squash-racket. He must have snatched it up from his extensive armoury of bats and balls and whatever as being a likely weapon with which to meet this obscure emergency.

'A most deplorable thing. A great loss to English archaeology.'

Bobby turned round. The voice was the voice of Dr Gulliver. He was wearing his academic gown, which gleamed greener than ever in the moonlight.

'And without doubt the most important of all the antiquities within reach of the school.' Dr Gulliver looked with the greatest severity at Bobby. Indeed, Bobby, who was still not quite himself, rather expected to be told that —displeasing as such a duty was—Dr Gulliver was obliged to correct him to the extent of two strokes with the cane. Fortunately, Dr Gulliver—with an agitated stride—simply moved away.

'Susan, what was the old ass talking about?'

'The Great Smithy. It was the Smithy they managed to concuss, and not the unconcussable Bobby Appleby. It was unsuspectedly unstable—as Beadon seemed to know. We found you'—Susan's voice suddenly trembled—'under the only chunk that still had a roof over it.'

'And those bearded chaps?'

'Buried. I suppose in what was a royal tomb. Ironic, in a way. Emissaries of a People's Republic, and so forth.'

'Yes.' Bobby looked, for the first time since getting to his feet, at the immediate scene of his recent romantic adventure. The giant caterpillar had crumpled up.

'Susan, people will be tumbling out of that helicopter?'

'At any moment.'

'And more arriving in cars? And there will have to be a fuss?'

'I suppose so. No Intelligence Service on earth could keep mum about an affair like this.'

'It's a marvellous moon. Look at the trunks of the beeches.'

'Fab.'

'Before all the chit-chat, we've time for a stroll to that nearest clump, don't you think?'

'I'm sure we have.'

And the great trees were around them when Solo's moon put on the last of its turns that night. As if snared in a bag, it vanished behind a stealthy and unsuspected cloud. Considering that it was in darkness that he had to do the job, Bobby took Susan very accurately in his arms.

'So there,' Bobby said. 'No more awkward lies.'